SLOW THE PACE

Anthology of Award-winning Short Stories

ISBN-10: 0-9851833-5-7
ISBN-13: 978-0-9851833-5-6

DEDICATION

This anthology is dedicated to those who know how to slow the pace

To the authors featured in this book: Scribes Valley thanks you for your time, patience, trust, and talent.
.

CONTENTS

SLOWING THE PACE
A Foreword by David L. Repsher, editor

They call it the Rat Race. The hustle, bustle, slam-bang pace of the world in which we live. *Rush, rush, rush* seems to be our motto, our credo, our way of life.

It can't be good for us. What is this hurry-up lifestyle doing to our bodies and minds? Sure, we may be getting ahead and "living the dream," but what is the cost? Shorter lifespans, ulcers, a general feeling of being worn out and frazzled? Aren't you supposed to like what you pay for?

Take the time to consider how your life is going. Are you part of the Rat Race? Personally, I can't stand anything to do with rats, so I try to avoid that way of life. I appreciate taking time out to enjoy the slower side of things. To be calm while surrounded by a world of chaos. To slow the pace of life and relish every second.

Slow the pace. Beautiful words. Words full of meaning and importance for all of us.

Step out of the Rat Race, let the rest of the world whiz on by. Allow yourself to sink into other worlds. Allow yourself to forget, to be carried away by the words contained in this anthology.

The rats can keep racing—they have for thousands, maybe millions of years—but *we* need to quit that race. We need to sit back, take stock of our lives, and definitely Slow the Pace.

FIRST PLACE

FOREVER AND ALWAYS
©2016 by Ronna L. Edelstein

Ronna dedicates "Forever and Always" to the memory of her beloved father, Morton M. Edelstein.

Had she known it was the beginning of the end, she might have handled things differently. She might have prepared Dad's favorite spaghetti—the kind that she poured into a pan, topped with cheese, and baked until the cheese looked like a bubbling yellow carpet. She might have cooked chili, another specialty that Dad loved. Even though Dad was not eating, the aromas emanating from the kitchen to his bedroom may have awakened pleasant memories in his addled brain.

She might have taken sick days from work so she could spend all day in the blue chair next to Dad's hospital bed, holding his hand, reading aloud to him from her book, watching *Law and Order: SVU* on television—Dad had a crush on Mariska Hargitay, the lead actress. She had heard that sound stayed with people, long after other senses disappeared. Maybe the sounds of the room—the sounds of her breathing—would bring comfort to Dad.

Had she known, she might have turned the chair next to Dad's bed into a makeshift bed. It would lack the comfort of her queen bed, but it would be close to Dad. She could listen to him breathe in person, not having to rely upon the baby monitor she had set up in his room and hers. If, by some miracle, he woke up and talked in a way that made sense, even for a few seconds, she would be there.

But Vera had refused to believe it was the beginning of the end. She had turned a deaf ear to the at-home hospice nurses who predicted "a week to ten days, but probably less than a week." She had pretended to not notice that Dad had stopped eating his favorite breakfast of scrambled eggs, toast drowning in jelly, and coffee—two cups, more cream than coffee. He had refused his night snack of ice cream, and he had a hard time swallowing any pills, forcing Vera to turn to the liquid medicine the hospice supplied. Vera tried to ignore how Dad slept all day; he lay on his right side, his right arm under his head, his left hand holding the rails of the hospital bed. Did he understand that those rails protected him from falling, or did he view them as prison bars that prevented him from living his life? She hoped that the morphine gave him pleasant dreams—or took all dreams away from him and left him in a state of peace.

Vera had spent that last week going about her business, as Grandma used to say. She awoke every morning before her alarm buzzed at 6 a.m. Vera needed time to do her morning ablutions before tending to Dad. "Ablutions" was Dad's word for his morning routine. Vera had adopted it because she liked the way it rolled off her tongue and how the second syllable made her lips come together as if she were about to whistle. She took her time brushing her teeth, reading the newspaper, and eating her cereal because she knew this was the calm before the emotional and physical storm. Once she went into Dad's room, she would no longer be Vera, independent woman and loving daughter, but Vera, caregiver, parent to her parent—but always-loving daughter.

During those last 168 hours of Dad's life, Vera never knew what to expect. Sometimes Dad was—and Vera hated the term but it seemed so apt—dead weight. She struggled to change his diaper that he had wet and dirtied in the night. She wore gloves as a caregiver would to protect her hands from germs, but the gloves made her feel dishonest as a daughter. What kind of daughter erects a barrier between her hands and her dad's skin? For all of her sixty-seven years, she had had a father who held her hand—literally and symbolically—to lead her down the roads of her life. Dad was a hugger and kisser; germs would not keep him from letting his skin connect with hers.

She cleaned Dad, something her "real" father would never have allowed. She shaved him because, even as his body slowly stopped functioning, his facial hair continued to grow. Vera wondered if she would have groomed him, even giving him a manicure and pedicure, if she had allowed herself to accept that he would not be attending a dinner party but would only be keeping an unwanted date with death.

Mother Nature treated the drama occurring within the small bedroom of the apartment with cruelty. She decided to have the sun smile from the time it awakened in the East until it settled down for its nightly snooze in the West. The temperatures felt more like a balmy July than a typical blustery October. If things had been different—Vera considers "if" as the most hateful word in the language, next to "death"—she would have taken Dad for a walk in his deluxe Rock 'n Roll wheelchair—the wheelchair that looked like a reclining easy chair on wheels. She would have wheeled him around the neighborhood, through the park, and past the yogurt store where, despite her daily gobbling of pounds of M&Ms due to stress, she would have treated herself and Dad to a dish of yogurt—chocolate for him and vanilla for her. Maybe she would have added sprinkles to hers and nuts to Dad's. Had she known what would soon occur, she would have doubled the size of Dad's yogurt with a huge swirl of whipped cream and the traditional cherry on top.

One hundred sixty-eight hours decreased to 144 hours; those hours raced to seventy-two hours as if the hands on the clock were in collusion with death to reach zero hour. With every passing minute, Dad seemed to shrink under his thin, yellow-and-white-striped sheet. He had been a large man, a six-footer with a muscular build. Ma used to tease him about his "short, fat neck," stating that it made it harder for her to buy him well-fitting shirts. Vera never joined the teasing because she saw Dad as perfect—as the father who went to work late on a Monday morning so he could take her to the nearby Five 'n Ten to buy her an outfit for one of her dolls; as the father who marched into her elementary school in an era when parents did not confront teachers to demand that the music teacher stop embarrassing Vera by making her sing alone; as the father who took her to dinner and a movie as a way to forget that no classmate had brought her a corsage and taken her to prom; as the father who held her hand and walked her down the aisle and, thirteen years later, again held her hand and walked her through divorce.

Dad had shrunk, not just in height but also in overall size. He seemed tiny, almost child-like in his hospital bed. In the early morning, the sun highlighted his diminished state by casting its rays upon him. By afternoon, however, Dad lay in shadows, a reminder of Psalm 23, Dad's favorite. Did Dad realize he had begun his walk through the valley of the shadow of death? Did he see a bright light, or did a thick wall of darkness loom before him?

Although neither Dad nor Vera was a religious person, they did pray—hoping that time would not change the life they enjoyed together—but they also understood that change would occur and that their days of walking, sitting in the park and reading, going to dinner and movies, and strolling through the mall would end. They knew that time was not generous to a man in his 90s; time would not slow down or stand still to allow that man—and his daughter—to continue forever and always, the words both Vera and Dad used when begging death to allow them to stay together—forever and always.

Vera sat alone with Dad. She had dismissed the current caregiver early, wanting to have a few hours with Dad before the next caregiver arrived. She sat on the blue chair next to the hospital bed and wondered what thoughts, if any, Dad had. She tried to talk to him about all they had shared, but she choked on the words. Instead, she held his hand and stared at him, trying to memorize the round shape of his face, the way his lips curled into a smile even when he slept, the chocolate-colored eyes that lay beneath closed lids.

Then Brian came, one of many caregivers who would breeze in and out during the next three days: Brian and Brittany, Adam and Pam, Linda and Mary—an alphabet soup of names and a collage of faces. The caregivers helped Vera turn Dad and change his diaper; they kept vigil while she took a quick nap. Most of all, they gave her someone with whom to dialogue. Vera welcomed the conversation, especially since her time with Dad was a monologue with her speaking and him—she did not know whether he heard or comprehended her words. But with the caregivers, she could discuss the latest breaking news, the loss or victory of the home team, the weather, and the early predictions for the 2016 presidential campaign. She could pretend that the caregivers were friends, not paid employees who were there only because Dad was declining and Vera could not do all the caring on her own.

Tim, the physical therapist, came, rubbing Dad's arms and massaging his legs, and turning him over so that he would not get bedsores. Randy, the occupational therapist, no longer came; Dad would not be needing help getting in and out of the car or lifting himself from his wheelchair to push the walker to the bathroom. Those days of so-called independence were already fading, like old photographs collecting dust at the bottom of a box in the attic. A different nurse—Faye, Shelley, George—stopped by every day to check Dad's vitals and to make sure he was getting enough morphine. Vera worried about giving him too much pain medication, but the nurses assured her that "too much morphine" did not exist at this point of time. Vera did not know whether those words comforted her since she did not want to harm Dad or caused her pain since they implied that hope no longer existed.

Yet, Vera continued to embrace hope. Every night she crawled into bed with a sleeping, almost comatose dad, and had cuddle time with him. "I love you the bestest and the mostest," she told him as she kissed his forehead and cheeks. "You sleep the greatest of anyone, and I'll see you tomorrow for breakfast. Maybe we'll take a walk in the hall if you feel like it."

Then, Vera would give Dad another kiss and rest her forehead against his lips for a pretend kiss from him. She would lie in her bed reading, but her tears would blur the words. Even when she could make out the letters, she would read without comprehension. Vera was using too much energy to battle reality. Her head, her mind, knew the truth—that the end was near—but her heart, her soul, refused to accept a world without Dad.

Chaplain Dave, a member of the in-home hospice team, came. While Vera and Dave did not share the same religion, they could still discuss pertinent questions about life and death. "What happens when we die?" Vera asked with a childlike innocence. She realized, as Dave searched for words, that all of his religious training had not made him any surer than the average lay person about what awaited mortals beyond life. Vera wanted Chaplain Dave to assure her that the afterlife existed, that heaven was a place filled only with sunshine. If there were stars, they shone during the day because heaven never experienced night. She imagined Dad, age ninety-eight, meeting his father, a man who died at age twenty-eight when Dad was not even three years old. Would the young father welcome the elderly son, or would he shy away from the old man his son had become? Would Ma and Grandma be waiting for Dad, or was every image of heaven a fairy tale that Vera needed to give her "once upon a time" life with Dad a "happily ever after" ending?

Vera fervently wanted to believe that Dad would join Ma and Grandma in this idyllic setting in which angels sang and danced and no one suffered. When Chaplain Dave said, "I don't know, but I believe there must be something after this life," Vera felt herself wanting to pummel the kindly minister with fists of frustration. Vera yearned for certainty, but the only certainty she received was that, within forty-eight hours at this point, Dad would discover for himself whether or not anything existed in death.

Occasionally, Dad would sit up in his hospital bed and start talking words that made no sense in a slurred speech that was hard to decipher. He used his arms to emphasize certain points that only he understood, and he became very agitated when neither Vera nor the caregiver of the hour could comprehend his meaning. Vera tried to calm Dad, holding his waving hand, telling him "it" would be okay. But Dad was not so easily fooled. He continued to speak the language of an anguished toddler; his eyes wandered from the dresser and chest-of-drawers he had purchased with Ma when they married seventy-five years earlier, to the pictures on the wall of him and Vera in Alaska, or of the two of them sitting on a bench overlooking the ocean in Atlantic City. His eyes then landed on Vera; they stared at her as if some part of Dad knew he would be leaving and he needed to have a precise picture of Vera to take with him.

During these semi-awake moments, Vera tried to get Dad to eat. "Have a banana," she coaxed. "The potassium is good for you." Dad looked at the banana as if he had never before seen the yellow fruit that he once had eaten on a daily basis. He looked at the oatmeal that he used to devour, the cup of chocolate pudding that he once adored, and the bottle of Ensure that he always had guzzled with such pleasure—he looked but he did not partake. That part of Dad that needed physical nourishment had died before death claimed all of Dad.

About thirty-six hours before the end, Vera stormed out of the apartment. She slammed the front door, not out of anger but out of frustration and fear. Instead of taking the elevator to the lobby, she chose to march down the three flights of stairs, pounding her feet against each step as if she could eradicate what was happening behind the closed door of the apartment. Vera went outside and, with an energy that belied her almost seven decades, began to jog down the street. She screamed as she jogged, oblivious to the stares of the other pedestrians and drivers who happened to look her way. She screamed at a system that gave people someone to love and then, with no logical reason, took that person away. She screamed at a world that was finite and at a death that was infinite. She, a senior citizen moving closer to her own mortality, screamed at time for turning her vital daddy, the man who had always been there for her, into the old man who lay asleep in the apartment in the hospital bed. Racing down the sidewalk, past the pole that Dad always touched for good luck, across the street that she and Dad had crossed a million times, Vera finally accepted the truth: Dad was going to die.

Resentment and rage filled Vera as she watched pedestrians engaging in conversations, sipping a large cup of coffee, or laughing at a comment someone made on their cell phone. How dare these people live their lives, oblivious of the dying taking place so nearby? Vera hated these people for their indifference to her pain; she hated the traffic lights for continuing to turn green, yellow, and red—for not having the compassion to stop on yellow to make everything and everyone, especially death, slow down. She suddenly remembered an Auden poem she had read in college: Icarus plunged from the sky into the sea, but the sun, not caring about this tragedy, still shone, and the unmindful ship and its crew still peacefully sailed on. That the world would keep spinning and people would keep living, despite the loss of Dad, seemed incomprehensible to Vera. A suffocating sense of aloneness and loneliness consumed her. With slow steps, as if her feet and legs no longer belonged to her, Vera trudged home— back to the blue chair, Dad, and the knowledge that she could do nothing but wait.

With thirty hours left, the nurse—the only health provider who refused to acknowledge that death was inevitable and lurking in a corner of the bedroom—came. "Do you see changes?" Vera could barely articulate the words. The nurse hesitantly nodded; Dad's skin was mottling, his diaper was dry from lack of urine output, his breathing seemed shallower. Yet, the nurse continued to avoid placing a time limit on Dad's life. "No one can predict," she insisted. But Vera again needed certainty. She did not want Dad to die, but she did not want the status quo to continue. She could not bear a life without Dad, but she could not bear a life with a Dad who was part-alive, part-dead—not in a vegetative state, but not alert and vibrant. Vera wanted time to fast forward, to get everything over with, and she wanted time to reverse, to return to several years earlier when Dad had been Dad, a man who could still find pleasure in food and books and television and "walks" in his wheelchair—joy in a meaningful albeit diminished life.

When Vera awoke on Friday, the last day in October, she again did her morning ablutions and headed for the blue chair next to Dad's bed. She talked to Dad about past Halloweens, in the "good ol' days" when children did not fear attacks by real monsters and when candy did not contain sharp needles or blades. She reminded Dad of how the two of them would trick or treat together, and how Dad would carry her bag when it became weighed down with treats. Once home, they would sort the candy into two piles: the wants and the not-wants. The not-wants they gave to Grandma to give to the children who shopped at her stepson's grocery store in a poor area of the city; the wants they kept so that Vera and Dad could have a daily treat for weeks and months to come.

The usual caregivers came and went that Friday, not knowing that they would have no further need to return. The nurse came around dusk; the look in her eyes confirmed for Vera that time was running out. Yet, even as she got into bed that night and checked to make sure the monitor was working, Vera was not prepared for what the middle of the night of November 1, 2014, would bring her.

A noise awoke her at 2 a.m. At first, Vera feared that someone—a burglar perhaps—had entered the apartment; she did not yet realize that the intruder was death. As the noise continued, however, Vera identified the sound as heavy, raspy breathing—the breathing of Boo Radley as he saved the lives of Jem and Scout from the diabolical Bob Ewell in *To Kill a Mockingbird*, Vera and Dad's favorite movie. Both slowly and quickly, Vera went to Dad's room, released the bars on one side of the bed, and crawled in next to him. Her left hand held his right as she began speaking to him, telling him she loved him and that it was okay to let go.

And the heavy breathing subsided. And the tension in Dad's body released. For thirty minutes, Vera lay next to Dad, holding him and speaking to him. "You were the first person to hold me when I was born," Vera whispered to him. "Your voice was the first I heard, your arms the first I felt, and your aroma the first I inhaled. And now my voice, touch, and smell are the last you will hear, feel, and sense." She leaned over Dad and kissed him—his forehead, his cheeks, his hands.

At 2:30 a.m., without any drama or fear, Dad took his last breath. Vera wrapped the sheet around him, trying to warm his already cooling skin. Then, in a daze, she called the hospice nurse and her children. She spoke the words "Dad" and "Grandpa" and "dead" in the same sentence, but nothing made sense to her. The clock in Dad's room continued to tick, the moon prepared for the rising of the sun, and the cars and buses still made noise on the street below.

The world moved forward, but Vera's world had ended. Death had claimed Dad, and loss had become Vera's new forever and always.

About the author:

As a part-time faculty member of the University of Pittsburgh's English Department, Ronna L. Edelstein works as a consultant at the school's Writing Center. She also teaches Freshman Programs, a course that introduces students to the University and the city. Her work, both fiction and nonfiction, has appeared in the following: "New Slang" A New Literary Voice by the Women and Girls of Pittsburgh" (online); *Quality Women's Fiction*; *Ghoti Online Literary Magazine*; *First Line Anthology*; *SLAB: Sound and Literary Artbook*; *Pulse: Voices from the Heart of Medicine* (online and print); *AARP Bulletin* (online and print); *Healthy Roots* (Forbes Health Foundation and Hospice); *The Jet Fuel Review* (Lewis University's online literary journal); Writer's Relief (online); *Seasons of Caring*; *Tales of Our Lives: Fork in the Road* (online e-book); *Signature* (Carnegie Mellon University Osher publication); *Verse Envisioned: the Poetry and Art of Pittsburgh*; the *Washington Post*; and the *Pittsburgh Post-Gazette*. "Forever and Always" is Ms. Edelstein's eighth Vera story to be honored by Scribes Valley Publishing.

Ronna dedicates "Forever and Always" to the memory of her beloved father, Morton M. Edelstein.

SECOND PLACE

SURVIVAL
©2016 by Jeff Spitzer

In the fall of 1975 I went camping with my father for the last time. I was ten years old and had no fear of the woods, but I dreaded these weekend trips. Father's moods, tortured by a badly ulcerated stomach—among other things—had been unpredictable all year. Our trips in June and September had ended bitterly, with both of us tense and silent because of our different priorities.

Father announced the late-October trip in his usual way: "Get your gear together, Danny. We're heading for the trees in the morning." His tone anticipated my full approval, and I knew better than to disappoint him. He was not a man who talked things over; he made swift, precise decisions and suffered no opposition. Had I dared to protest, he would have fired off sensible arguments, then accusations of weakness and sloth until I finally caved in.

By "the trees," Father meant the Wayne National Forest in southeastern Ohio, but not the groomed, well-trodden paths. We would roam, as he liked to quote, far from the madding crowd.

"The leaves will be fantastic now," he said in a voice too harsh and self-assured to be compatible with autumn beauty.

"Can Mom come?" I asked half-heartedly.

He ignored me and began sifting through a pile of his political leaflets. I didn't repeat the question because I already knew the answer. Father would not want Mother on the trip, and she, obligingly, would be too busy to go. My parents preferred to avoid each other. Their marriage had come apart years ago, but instead of divorcing they had given themselves over to radically different inspirations.

I went out the back door in sullen protest. Bosser, my English sheepdog, joined me in the meadow and we lost ourselves in high grass and wildflowers.

My parents and I lived a few miles from Proctorville in southern Ohio. Our house was tiny, but our backyard blended into a vast, wild meadow, which flowed out to a woods. Rabbits, raccoons, foxes, deer, and a variety of harmless snakes meandered across the landscape. Bobwhites and grouses shot up before a footstep. Bosser and I would roam far and wide without purpose while dozens of fantasies—childish adventures, secret devices, imaginary playmates—revolved in my head. Often I'd gaze for long minutes at an unfamiliar object until it seemed to take on a different nature. The outdoors was a relief, my daydreams a partial antidote to the tension that hovered in my home.

I had no close friends. Sometimes one of my classmates would spend an afternoon with us, but this was rare. The other boys called me "sleepwalker" and "space cadet." Their mothers had been warned by stories of my parents' peculiar interests.

My father taught biology at Proctorville High School. Every day of the school year he complained about lazy students, ignorant parents, or the bigoted principal. Father was a thin man with a receding hairline, a short beard, and wire-rimmed glasses. He always seemed to be in motion. Whenever he left the house he took along a Thermos of milk to soothe his ulcer. I knew that people in the area argued about him.

He traveled a lot. After school and all through the summer he drove to coal and steel towns along the Ohio River and in Kentucky and West Virginia. He returned in the evenings after Mother and I had eaten. Barely greeting us, he would descend to the basement, where he had a typewriter and mimeograph. For a couple of hours, I'd hear his index fingers tapping the keyboard and his occasional eruptions of mirthless laughter and swearing, as if a crowd of men were down there with him. I wasn't allowed downstairs while he worked, but I had seen him once at the typewriter. He sat hunched over, eyes aflame, his head bobbing repeatedly as he scrutinized every line.

Finally he would emerge with a stack of paper in his purple-stained hands and carry it out to his station wagon. His noisy old Ford had gone through several engines. The cargo area was carpeted with leftover fact sheets, position papers, newsletters, and manifestos, all in a chaotic weave, muddy, creased, and torn. These political statements sounded like battle cries:

End the war!
Freedom now!
Save the forests!

And others meant to rally the mine workers and steel workers against their bosses. The shrill boldface print used to scare me, even when I didn't understand the conflict.

***

The next day, as Father and I loaded our backpacks into the station wagon, Bosser padded up to me in his floppy, optimistic way. I scratched around his hairy face. I had always wanted to take him with us, but Father would not allow it. Bosser suffered from a hip dysplasia. Our kind of hiking would have been impossible for him.

Father closed the tailgate and told me to get in, but I pretended not to hear. "Are you coming?" he asked impatiently.

"Dad, I was thinking. If we stayed on the trail, Bosser would be all right."

"We're not going to stay on the trail. You know that."

"Just this once, can we?"

Mother came around the side of the house with herbs from her garden. She fussed over my clothes and looked in my backpack to make sure I had extra socks and underwear. She gave me a long hug and promised to bake cookies for me while we were gone. Then she cast a baleful glance at Father's back. "Don't wear him out," she warned.

He didn't bother to answer.

"Be careful, Daniel," she advised me with a look of concern, as if she, not he, were my true protector. Then, without any further communication, she trudged off to the house.

***

Mother was a tall, stout woman, whose hair had turned leaden gray before she was forty. Six days a week she wore loose-fitting sweatshirts, jeans, and blue canvas shoes. Sundays, when she and I went to church, she put on a green or blue dress, a fake pearl necklace, and pumps, which she dyed and re-dyed to match the dress. Like Father, she was always busy but in another room with her own tasks. The three of us spent most of our time in different places.

Mother worked around the house from sunrise until long after dinner; cooking, sewing, cleaning, paying the bills, doing most of the yard work, repairing everything from squeaky drawers to leaky pipes. One summer, in 95-degree heat, she put a new roof on the house by herself.

"Your father can't be bothered with honest work," she often said under her breath.

She took no interest in Father's political activities and never read his literature. She had reading material of her own. Every week pamphlets addressed to Mother appeared in our mailbox. They came from everywhere and nowhere and ended their journey on neat piles in her bedroom closet. There were pocket-sized *Daily Devotionals* with flowers, birds, and sunsets on the covers. Square green *Triumphs* and rectangular *Messengers* had pictures of Jesus, the saints, and little children. Deeper inside her closet were *The Candles* with their unevenly printed pages, too faint in some places and smudged in others. Mother read alone in her room after putting me to bed. Even though her door was closed, I knew she was frowning in her doily-draped armchair under a yellow lamp.

Once a day she recited something called decrees. Decrees were an odd way of praying that few people knew about. Alone at the kitchen table she would call out a list of commands: "Angelic hosts, come forth and blaze your mighty rays of light through all," she'd intone to the spotless cupboards. "Purify our hearts with your violet flame. Lift us to the light. Fill

22

us with the light."

On the back steps, gazing over the wild grass toward the tree line, she would raise her muscular arms and cry: "In Archangel Michael's love and name, by the power of his sword, use your holy energy to raise the earth to her God-estate!"

She might repeat each decree twenty or thirty times and then begin another one. She read them from *Triumph*. The whole list took almost half an hour.

I was eight years old when she began reading decrees. I found her in the kitchen one day calling out to the angels of Saint Germain, repeating the same strange words over and over. Terrified, I ran out of the house and buried my face in Bosser's shaggy fur.

Later she explained it to me. "Angels are all around us," she said. "They hold the mighty power of God. If you're very quiet and listen with your heart instead of your ears, you can hear their voices. When I feel their presence, I must direct their power to bring about good things like health and peace and love. Decrees help to focus God's power on the needs of our world."

I nodded my head.

"But decrees take my full concentration," she went on. "You mustn't interrupt me."

I shook my head.

"Don't be frightened, Daniel."

"I won't."

"And one more thing. You mustn't talk to your father about this. Okay?"

"Okay." It must have seemed normal to me that adults should have their secrets. Or maybe I sensed that Father wouldn't care much about angels and decrees. At any rate I kept silent for almost two years.

I sometimes heard angels myself. At night they would enter my dreams, muttering all around me in harsh, murky voices. I couldn't see them or understand their words, but I feared they wanted to kill me. When I cried out to them in peace, they refused to listen and their senseless voices grew louder. I'd wake up in terror and run to Mother's bedside.

"Stop it! Stop it!" she'd hiss, afraid that the sound of my sobbing might penetrate Father's bedroom. "You didn't hear angels. You had a bad dream."

She would steer me back to my room and groan, "Oh, Daniel, not again," when she saw that I'd wet my bed. She'd change my sheets in weary silence while I put on new pajamas. She wouldn't let me touch her. "Go to sleep," she'd say. "No more nonsense. I'm too tired."

Mother sewed my clothes, gave me haircuts and drove me to and from school in her VW bus. She fed me balanced meals with a vitamin pill beside my plate. At bedtime she made sure I said my prayers. Somehow, though, she attended my needs without giving me much of her attention. I seemed to be one more item on her long list of chores.

***

As soon as I got into the station wagon, I noticed a little hole in the windshield, right between the wipers. Straight crack lines radiated from the hole in almost perfect symmetry. I stuck my finger through it as Father climbed in the driver's side.

"Danny, get away from that!"

"What did it?"

"I don't know what did it. Just leave it alone."

"Did a rock do it?"

"I told you I don't know. Yeah, maybe a rock did it."

"Did someone throw a rock at you?"

"Will you drop the matter, damn it!"

I sulked against the door. Father didn't say a word as we drove out to the highway. His surly gaze spanned a hundred miles. I had a feeling this trip would be as dreary as the others.

Father knew many places in the Wayne National Forest, which extends over eleven Ohio counties. We went south through Proctorville, where we passed our schools and drove for an hour on narrow, hilly roads. Sometimes the Ohio River came into view. In one town we stopped at a traffic light, and Father spoke for the first time.

"Remember that building over there, the steel mill? They're laying off a hundred men."

I looked at the smoking jungle of gray structures. I counted seven tall smokestacks. One of the little cars was climbing the long track to the top of the blast furnace. It dumped its load and started down again. I imagined myself riding on the car to the top and then diving into an empty vat but never hitting bottom. The light changed, and we headed out of town.

"Are you going to get laid off?" I asked.

He glanced at me sharply. "No, of course not. I'm a teacher, not a steelworker." He pulled down a veil of gloom, and I wished I hadn't blurted out such a stupid question. The steelworkers were suffering and I couldn't find anything intelligent to say. I gazed at the hole and crack lines. They kept turning into a cat's face. In my mind I asked the cat why anyone would throw a rock at our car. Before it came up with an answer we entered a yellow blur of autumn trees.

***

Somewhere in the forest, Father turned onto a lonely dirt road. We bounced over ruts until we came to a stretch of grassy berm. Father stopped the car, and we unloaded our things and ate our bologna sandwiches. It was a clear, sunny day, but a chill was seeping into the air. I had on a black tee shirt with the peace symbol, my Pirates cap, knee-worn jeans, and hiking boots.

"You remembered to bring a sweater, right?" Father said.

I mumbled a reply. My pack contained some Mexican coins, a jackknife, extra socks and underwear, a flashlight, and two comic books. I imagined that somehow a sweater had been sucked from the floor of my closet into my pack. My sleeping bag had always kept me warm, and maybe I'd never need a sweater.

Father tied a red bandana around his forehead. He wore a khaki tee shirt, camouflage pants, and hiking boots. The treads in his boots were almost gone. After we strapped on our packs he said, "Okay, let's move out."

As we slipped through an opening in the woods, I worried that Father would soon be angry with me. I tried to recall our last trip. We had camped out on the Labor Day weekend, somewhere else in the Wayne Forest. Everything was green then, and all three days were hot and muggy. At night it rained. Now the air was dry with a scent of fallen leaves, and it was turning cold. Red and gold color surrounded us. The forest had changed, and I couldn't remember Father's lessons.

I followed him through dead, viny underbrush that made me think of Halloween skeletons. We scrambled up a hill and picked our way through billowing green laurel. A fallen log was covered with patches of white fungi. I stopped to feel them. Lace doilies made of rubber, I thought, and the idea amused me.

"Danny!" Father shouted, and I ran to catch up with him.

When we emerged on a flat meadow, I remembered one of his lessons: Erosion—trees stopped erosion. Their dead leaves kept rainwater from washing away the soil. But logging companies cut down the trees. Oil drillers knocked them down with bulldozers. Greedy people were destroying the earth.

I went over it again. Erosion. Dead leaves. Greedy logging companies and drillers. The earth would get destroyed. I hoped that Father would ask me about erosion. We descended a gentle slope by the edge of a ravine. Below I could see the tops of evergreens. Across the chasm were outcroppings of sandstone covered with moss and ferns that looked like a green waterfall. I heard the scream of a hawk.

Father marched straight ahead with his eyes on the ground. In his khaki shirt and camouflage pants he reminded me of soldiers on TV, but he had never been in the Army; he cursed at the soldiers in Vietnam. In the woods, as at home, he seemed to know exactly what he was doing and where he was going. He'd forge ahead with a fierce glare in his eyes, the same expression he wore when he typed his papers. He avoided the trails. As he put it, "You run into everybody. Jerks with cameras, kids goofing off, and old ladies rattling on about their grandchildren."

The hawk and the green waterfall caught my attention, and I fell behind again.

"Danny, for the last time, quit your daydreaming!" Father yelled.

I ran to him. No way would I be one of those goof-off kids.

He suddenly changed direction. We moved away from the ravine and into the trees. Father sat down on a log. "Okay, Danny, take off your pack."

He helped me squirm out of the straps. I repeated to myself: Trees stop erosion. Loggers. Drillers. The earth would be destroyed.

He looked at his watch. "I want you to find me two edible plants. You've got three minutes."

Edible plants! That was the other lesson. I glanced around the forest floor, but every shrub and weed looked the same. I stood there paralyzed, as if waiting for some plant to raise its hand.

"Two minutes."

I tore and sniffed. I touched my tongue to the tips of leaves.

"One minute. Come on now, think! What part of the plant would you eat? Think about color."

Hopelessly confused, I pulled on a long, trailing vine that was still producing white flowers. The roots came out easily. I wound the vine into a coarse spool and took it to Father.

"What's this?" he said with a look of distress. "You want to eat *this*?"

I shrugged and stared at the ground. He tossed the wretched plant behind him.

"I should *make* you eat that thing," he said. "Don't you remember anything we talked about?"

"I remember about erosion."

"That's fine but I'm talking about survival now. What if you were alone in the woods and it was a question of eating or dying? Where would you be after the first week?"

Not wanting to answer, I just scuffed my toe on the log.

"Dead as dog shit, right?" He made me stand still. "Right?"

I nodded, keeping my eyes lowered.

"Can you find me *one* edible plant in thirty seconds?" When I made no reply he said, "Danny, what's growing two feet in back of me? Will you look, please? This is important."

A blizzard of green was all I saw through my moist eyes. Father reached behind him, yanked out an evergreen shrub, and held it under my nose. He pointed, in descending order, to four red berries. "Do you remember its name?"

I didn't.

"Partridgeberry. Say it. Partridgeberry." I mumbled the word with him. "Here," he said, "eat one." We each chewed up and swallowed a berry. "Not much taste but it could save your life."

I hoped we were finished. I still couldn't meet his eyes.

"All right, that's one. Now study the trees around us, especially the bark."

The instant he mentioned bark, I remembered the shaggy hickory tree. I spotted one and plowed through the brush toward it. Dried husks were scattered all over the ground. I pried out the nuts and, supporting them against my chest, carried as many as I could back to Father.

"Let's crack them open," I said.

"We don't have time. Just leave them here and we'll move on."

He stood up. I let the nuts fall, and Father helped me strap on my pack. While he worked behind me I gazed sadly at the nuts. I wondered if I could really crack them open. Father might be pleased if we had them for supper.

"Let's go," he said.

I quickly stuffed two handfuls of nuts into my jeans. We continued down the slope beside the ravine. Soon I heard the hiss of moving water.

A wide stream rushed beneath a canopy of leaves. The joyful water made me laugh, as I did when Bosser licked my chin after school. Father relaxed his pace, and we ambled along the bank in search of a campsite. I felt a need to talk to him but didn't know how to begin. If I didn't think of something, he would probably start another lesson.

"Dad, do you ever hear angels?"

"What?" His initial look of surprise turned into one of suspicion.

"Do angels talk to you sometimes?"

"Talk to me? No, they don't. And who's been talking to you? Your mother?" He glowered at me.

I was shocked that he knew. I had not intended to divulge Mother's secret but only to bring up the general subject of angels. Now I felt that I had betrayed her.

"Has she been filling your head with that rubbish?" Father demanded.

Again I avoided his eyes.

He lowered his pack to the ground. "We'll camp here," he said crossly. "Take off your pack."

I obeyed instantly.

Father paced back and forth, gathering steam. Then he stood over me while I hung my head.

"Danny, I'm going to tell you a few things and I want you to listen for once. We in America are fighting a new civil war. You remember that hole in the windshield? That wasn't a rock. It was a bullet! Yes, it shocked me too, but it shouldn't have. We're in a war against greedy, powerful men who ruin people's lives and destroy the earth. But now the little people are waking up. For years I've fought oppression and destruction, and I want you to take up the fight someday. But, Danny, you can only win if you understand what the war is about and proceed according to a sensible plan, like an army. You must learn and then act. You cannot waste time daydreaming. Gods and angels are just daydreams, Danny. They're fantasies of weak, fearful people. You've never seen an angel and neither has anyone else. You can't survive on dreams."

When Father grew this agitated, I knew it was futile to speak. So I stood there beneath the hail of his wrath until he finished. Then I traced a circle with my toe while he set our packs under a tree, wiped his glasses, and shakily turned the pages of his field guide. Suddenly, he sat down on a rock and pressed one hand into his lower chest. His attacks of ulcers began like this.

He found his Thermos, poured a little milk into the cap, and gulped it. Pressing his chest again, he breathed deeply and wiped his face and beard with his bandana. When the pain finally subsided, he looked confused and embarrassed. As I watched him from the corner of my eye, I felt relieved because the attack would redirect his thoughts.

The sky had clouded over and the temperature had dropped a few more degrees. It was late in the afternoon. We had not seen another soul for hours. Father started to unravel the tent but changed his mind.

"Let's leave this for now," he said. "I want to show you some things before it gets dark."

He led me up the bank. Every few yards he stopped to point out signs of life. He showed me the remains of larvae on the bottom of rocks that he pulled from the stream. He talked about flies and beetles that live under water sometimes for years until they turn into adults. Names and facts poured out of him. Larval stages, nymphs, life cycles. Insect A was prey to insect B. Insect B lived this long as a nymph and that long as an adult. One swam on its belly, another on its back, still another had split eyes that could see above and below the water.

Father plunged his hand into the stream and pulled out a crawdad. Holding it in the middle with his fingertips, he pointed out the antennae, claws, tail, and the five pairs of legs. "If one leg is lost, he just grows another. He can flip his tail down and swim backwards to avoid danger. The first order of business in nature is survival."

That was today's lesson: survival. Father kept repeating the word and made sure I appreciated that all the strange characteristics of these creatures were meant to support their existence.

"Humans have to survive also," he went on. We were wading in the shallow stream, ostensibly in search of more animals, but Father's attention had shifted. "We're in a never-ending war with our own species. They're already combing these forests for oil and gas. One day, if we let them, they'll turn the whole country into a desert."

They trampled on helpless people around the world. They polluted the air and water, brainwashed the citizens, and fired their workers to increase their profits. We had to stop them *now*.

In the midst of his passion, he doubled over, fell into the water, and staggered onto the bank. He began rubbing his chest and side. Grunting in pain, he started back toward the campsite and immediately dropped to his knees.

"Danny," he whispered, clutching his side.

As I scrambled onto the bank, he crawled toward a massive oak tree a few yards away. I hadn't realized how far upstream we had come.

When I looked for our campsite, and Father's precious milk, I saw only a darkening landscape thick with misshapen trees and ominous foliage. The din of the water seemed to have risen up and formed a ghostly presence. *The angels of my nightmares are coming for us*, I thought. They were angry with me for betraying Mother and with Father for his blasphemy.

I ran to him. He was retching violently and he waved me away. Something red and horrible fell out of his mouth. Part of it stuck to his beard, and he flung it off in disgust. Waves of pain and nausea swept through him, as if chunks of his insides were being scorched away. He tried to stand but toppled onto his side, gasping and drawing up his knees, expelling loud farts between the moans. I was scared to death. His attacks had never lasted so long, and there had never been blood. But the worst part came when he began growling, cursing, and writhing insanely. He seemed to be locked in mortal combat with an invisible opponent.

At last he collapsed against the big tree. His eyes gazed helplessly upward. I approached him slowly and noticed a change: a softer cast to his eyes, a relaxing of his facial muscles, a frail smile dappled with sweat. Had I ever seen him smile?

He was looking at me in a different way, with mildness and affection. He tried to reach out to me, but his strength was gone. A feeble hissing sound emerged from his mouth. Leaning over, I heard him repeat the words "son...son..." I wiped his face with his bandana, and he brushed his lips against my fingers. I knelt beside him. Our heads were on the same level, and I let him look at me as I stared deeply into his eyes.

He seemed to have thrown off a terrible burden. Long afterward, I imagined that the madding crowd of bosses, drillers, loggers, and soldiers—the dark angels of my father's dreams—had retreated, leaving me in the open, visible for the first time.

"I'll get the Thermos," I said and, with a resolution that astonished me, I raced downstream completely forgetting my phantom terrors. I leaped over rocks, logs, and roots and splashed in and out of the water where the bank narrowed. A cold, heavy, moonless twilight had settled in. The forest was still. I liked the reassuring feel of the chilly, calf-high water as it soaked my pants and seeped into my tightly laced boots.

I found the Thermos in Father's pack, but in my haste and exhilaration I neglected to take anything else, not even our food or a flashlight. I fled back upstream, clutching the Thermos under my shirt as if exposure to the air might spoil its contents. On the way, I thought about the hickory nuts in my pockets and was proud of my foresight.

Father was barely awake. He acknowledged my triumphant return with a faint smile and a touch, the finest rewards I had ever known.

"You drink it," he whispered, as I held the cup to his lips.

"But, you're sick."

He shook his head weakly. "No. You need to drink it."

At that moment, I think, I knew he was dying. But the possibility of his death was too much to dwell on, so I found a rock and cracked open the nutshells, collecting their meager fruit in my baseball cap. Again Father declined to eat.

"Good boy," he said. "Eat them all. Tomorrow maybe you can find more."

I chewed up the tasteless nuts. It was quite cold now, and I realized we should get out of our wet clothes. The ground was covered with leaves. In the final minutes of daylight I carried armloads of leaves to the oak tree, pulled off Father's boots and pants, removed my own, and buried us in a dry, crunchy blanket. I planned to fetch our gear in the morning, pitch the tent, start a fire, and cook our food. Father would direct me and I would carry out every task and not waste time daydreaming. Snuggled up against him, feeling the coarse hair of his limbs, I hardly thought of home and safety. The forest was our perfect home, and we were safe in each other's arms.

For three days he clung to life. Most of the time he lay unconscious; occasionally his breathing grew labored and his eyes fluttered open, as if he had struggled up from a chasm to make sure I was okay. He couldn't communicate. He probably never saw the tent and the fire. But when I showed him my capful of partridgeberries, which I had spent the day gathering, I caught the faint flicker of a smile and knew he was pleased. Now I had to survive. If I did, he and Mother would be pleased together.

That made a pleasant daydream as I kept the fire going, dried our clothes, and tried to stay warm. On the fourth day I was rescued by members of a search party, who had spotted the station wagon and fanned out toward the streams. Father had died. They found me huddled against him, shivering and debilitated, murmuring to Bosser as I did at home. One man thought my mouth was bleeding, but it was only juice from the berries.

About the author:

Jeff Spitzer lives in Columbus, Ohio near his two grown children and four grandchildren. His story "The Last Ordeal of James Willoughby" won 3rd prize in the 2014 Scribes Valley contest. Besides that, his short stories have appeared in several small-press and college magazines such as *The Sun*, *Cimarron Review*, and *Louisiana Literature*.

THIRD PLACE

INTERIOR DESIGNS
©2016 by Dorene O'Brien

Sure I took the assignment. Did I have a choice? I'd just started with Dyer & Bramble, the largest design firm east of the Mississippi, and I would have viewed *any* task as laudable. I was by far the youngest decorator they'd ever hired and had adopted a stray dog mentality toward my superiors: *You can abuse me as long as you keep me.*

Vicki Gunsky and Rebecca DeNikers had already refused the assignment, but that didn't necessarily mean the assignment was bad. After all, they're famous—they even have their own cable show— each with a flock of clients that keeps them hopping between all-expense paid sushi lunches and crab salad dinners. Klauss Wilms had also refused the assignment, but who knew about him? Klauss walked around the office in straw hats, Hawaiian shirts and khaki shorts. He seldom spoke, and I don't remember ever seeing him with a client, although he had no compunction about using the glass-walled client conference room to eat his whole-wheat bagels. He was an icon, pure and simple, someone who had *arrived*. Klauss dressed ridiculously, ignored most of us and refused assignments with impunity. And we all wanted to be him. I cannot imagine the amount of confidence it must take to wear those shirts around a group of people who are in the business of making fashion judgments.

So I jumped at the chance to take an assignment that had been refused by the best; I figured they would recall their refusals with regret when they read the reviews in *Interiors Today*: "Jenna Matthews, young upstart with mature skills, forges futuristic work space," "Child decorator captures the attention of big design hot shots," "Modest decorator credits company veterans who mentored her." Maybe they'd even get a quote from Klauss who, of course, would have to make something up.

The noble assignment: revamping several roadside ice cream parlors owned by a wealthy eccentric named J.M. Krommer. Mr. Dyer took the client not only because he was rich, but because his grandson and Krommer's nephew were best friends, who were at the time utterly enamored of the Krommer Bomber, an F-35 shaped ice cream packaged in collectible wrappers. I doubted that these boys were studying market trends during ice cream binges and felt Mr. Dyer's trust in their product instinct was ill-conceived, but who was I to question him?

"Throw a package together, Matthews," he said. "He wants Air Force, we'll give him Air Force. Bombers, airplanes. No more clowns and balloons. We're appealing to the sophisticated child."

"Mr. Dyer—" and I should say here that this was the extent of my vocalized concern about the design.

"This could lead to big things, Matthews. He's got stores all over. This could really take off. Get it? Take off?"

"That's very funny, sir," I yipped.

I was, as I suggested, somewhat uneasy about the assignment—weren't today's kids more interested in video game stars, Pixar characters, LEGOs?—but I located some fighter jet wallpaper, posters depicting flying aces from classic movies and framed pictures of Sikorsky H-19s and B-52 scramble take-offs. I designed an ice cream dispenser overlay shaped like an F-35 instrument panel, the dispensing arm replaced by a throttle, and during the presentation I'd prepared for Krommer I recommended the company rename the desserts to reflect the new theme: Tailspins, Kamikazes, Flight Zone Cones. Mr. Dyer frowned, but I buzzed along, suggesting that hostesses wear lightweight helmets and that the company consider biplane rides for be-goggled kids as a promotional event. Mr. Dyer's eyes widened as I held forth on jet-shaped ice cream containers, seat-belted picnic tables with overhead umbrellas replaced by billowing parachutes, ideas flying from my mouth before having made a full revolution through my head. Finally Mr. Krommer held his right hand up in the STOP position. I sank onto my chair, Klauss's chair, conscious of the bagel crumbs burrowing into the nap of my wool skirt, and watched Krommer's eyes search the ceiling, his thumb circling his temple in the headache relief gesture.

"I can see it," he said. "I can see it."

Mr. Dyer wrinkled his forehead and the downward arc of his eyebrows told me that he, too, was working feverishly to interpret Krommer's statement.

"I love it," said Krommer, looking at me. "I think we have a deal, Major. But I must first consult Sedgewick."

"Fine," I said. "Of course."

Dyer was all smiles when Krommer left, but I was worried. "Who's Sedgewick?" I asked, unnerved by the prospect of a sane man reviewing my proposal.

Dyer snapped his briefcase shut and said, "His nephew."

Sedgewick's blessings were promptly attained and we began work immediately on the three largest stores.

"They are the jewels in my crown," said Krommer. "The changes will be most noticed there. How's that sound, Major?"

"Great," I said, pooling the spit I had gathered on my tongue to pop several Tylenol when he turned his back.

Krommer showed up each day to supervise, strewing forth military titles with abandon. "Watch the tiles there, Private, those are five bucks apiece" or "Good morning, Captain, how about a Bomb Pop, compliments of the old commander?" or "These fellas are the Green Berets of plaster, don't you think, Major?"

"Yes," I said. "They're trying to be."

I also noted with a combination of annoyance and resignation Krommer's constant use of the word *we* as if he had, by his unrelenting presence, become part of Dyer & Bramble. *We* worked for several weeks on the three stores simultaneously and were making such rapid progress that Krommer announced he would be bringing his wife, Eunice, to see the Laurel Street store, his favorite.

"I'd like you to be there," he said, "in case she has any questions."

"Of course."

"It's a surprise," he said, index finger poised vertically over his lips. "I've had to keep quiet for weeks. Can you imagine?"

"No."

"Her father was a pilot in WW two. She'll be tickled. But not to mention ice cream," he warned.

"Excuse me?"

"She hates the stuff. And if you don't mind too much," he added, "I'd like to tell her the ideas were mine." He kicked at a loose floor tile. "Okay, General?"

"Certainly," I said.

I arrived early the day Eunice Krommer was to visit, too agitated to eat breakfast and, although my excitement was tempered by her husband's appropriation of my ideas, I was eager for her reaction, hungry for applause from someone other than my loopy client. Mr. Dyer arrived as I was unwrapping a Fudgsicle.

"Good morning," he said, staring at the ice cream as if I were unveiling a severed finger.

"I didn't have breakfast, and Mr. Krommer said it was okay," I said, covering all possible grounds for his disapproval. He waved my words away and looked around.

"Looks good, kid. Eunice will love it. Don't worry," he added as if reading my mind, "she's not nearly as wacky as her old man."

Krommer's New Yorker pulled up moments later, and Mr. Dyer turned to me and smiled. "Good luck," he said.

"Thanks."

"Better not let Eunice see that," he added, nodding at my half-eaten Fudgsicle.

Through the plate-glass window I watched Krommer help his wife out of the car and across the parking lot, maneuvering her past paint cans and cement barrels with great speed and dexterity. It wasn't until she tripped over a small pile of lumber and hit the pavement with both knees that I realized she was blindfolded.

Krommer helped her up and he and Mr. Dyer escorted her into the building, each grasping an arm of what was to all appearances a befuddled rag doll, knees bloody and blindfold askew. She perched on a small wooden stool and I asked if I could get her a glass of water. She pulled off the blindfold and squinted at me.

"Have you been eating ice cream?" she asked.

Krommer shot Mr. Dyer an angry look, surely blaming him for my indiscretion much the same way a parent chastises a negligent babysitter.

"Of course not," I said.

"What's that on your mouth?"

"Danish," I said. "Chocolate danish."

She turned to Krommer. "Well, it's about time you started serving something other than that awful ice cream in here. Is that the surprise?"

Krommer laughed. "Look around, Eunice. See the wallpaper?" He pointed to the ice cream dispenser. "Wanna play with the throttle?"

Eunice Krommer stood slowly and surveyed her husband's favorite ice cream shop.

"Oh, my," she said, a bloodied napkin pressed to her chest. "What have you done?"

"We've fixed 'er up," said Krommer. "This here's the new Krommer theme. Bombers, parachutes, flying aces." He waved his arm in a semicircle and said, "It was *my* idea."

Eunice Krommer leaned wearily against the faux F-35 overlay. "Well," she said, "I'm not surprised."

Eunice Krommer's disapproval translated into several things: a new design featuring—oh, the irony—clowns and balloons, the histrionics of Mr. Sedgewick Krommer, and my first lesson in bending the capriciousness of human nature to my advantage. I was more surprised than unsettled by the shock on Mr. Dyer's face when Eunice Krommer insisted that a war zone was no place for a child to eat ice cream and that her father, a decorated military veteran, would spin in his grave if he knew her own husband was luring children into his twisted web of violence with confections.

When it became clear that Eunice Krommer would win, I said, "We can have this replaced by next month."

"Finally," she said, "a voice of reason."

She then turned to her husband, who looked both bewildered and devastated, and said, "I *do* like the danish idea, though."

When the Krommers left, Mr. Dyer turned to me and said, "I told you she was a nutcase, didn't I?"

"Yes, sir, you did."

"An ice cream magnate that hates the very thing that keeps her in T-bone steaks and New Yorkers."

"That is a riddle," I said.

"Throw something together, Matthews. Clowns, balloons, the whole freaking big top. I don't care. Suggest elephant rides, monkeys serving banana splits. They're crazy enough to go for it. Just finish the job and get them out of my hair."

"Yes, sir," I said. "I can do that."

Mr. Dyer stormed out and I opened the cooler to retrieve my Fudgsicle. "Hey, Ensign," I called to the electrician, "how 'bout a Nutty Buddy?"

"No, thanks," he muttered without turning from his work.

"Suit yourself," I said, taking both the Fudgsicle and the Nutty Buddy. They may not have been the five-star meals or designer dresses Lansky and DeNikers received, but they were perks just the same.

And so the Krommer assignment began my career as a weathervane, blowing easily in the direction I figured would most reward me. I didn't make a decorating move without first consulting Eunice Krommer, and I listened calmly as she berated Mr. Dyer for not returning her calls. I won her trust and respect simply by entertaining her decorating notions, by nodding innocently as she made it clear she did not comprehend the convoluted mechanism of the corporate infrastructure.

"*You* should be running that company," she said. "You're talented, cooperative and wise beyond your years. Why, you should be the

CEO."

Throughout the assignment, all Mr. Dyer ever said to me was, "Get them out of my hair," after which Klauss would wink at me while shooting his finger. I don't know if he was reiterating Mr. Dyer's command or suggesting I kill the Krommers, but either way he'd finally acknowledged my existence. I'd smile, but I could never bring myself to shoot back.

I did a remarkable job with the Krommer account, considering that I was taking orders from two lunatics who knew nothing about interior design. Sometimes I ignored their ideas, sometimes I kneaded them into the theme, and sometimes I implemented my own ideas disguised as theirs; they were always happy to take credit when the results looked good. I learned that humility is an important attribute in the design business. Still, I was as eager to get them out of my life as Mr. Dyer had been, so I worked tirelessly to finish the job.

One day when I was finishing up the final store, Klauss walked in and stalked the counter in his safari outfit, pith helmet and all.

"Tornado. Large. Heath bar." He shot his finger at me as I fixed a rubber elephant trunk to the cash register's change dispenser.

"Klauss," I said. "It's me."

He stared at me over the top of his Raybans. "You *work* here?"

"No," I sighed. "I'm on assignment," I said with the drama of a Russian spy.

He winked and said, "I'm in a bit of a rush. How about that Tornado?"

***

There were no five-page photo stories or glossy spreads of my work in *Interiors Today*, but the Krommers were pleased and Mr. Dyer, apparently thankful that I'd been able to keep them out of his life without killing them, invited me to one of the company dinners at La Chasse. Since these dinners were typically attended only by veteran employees, I saw this as my chance to network, to lick the hand of anyone I thought might throw me a bone. I bought a new dress and paid my stylist to coif my hair in a way that looked sexy but not slutty, unique but not professionally done.

I passed through the leather-padded front doors of La Chasse a few minutes late—I didn't want to appear eager—and saw Klauss and Mr. Dyer standing just inside at the bar. Under normal circumstances I probably wouldn't have noticed them, but Klauss was wearing an Indiana Jones hat with a large quail feather jutting across the side, and when he turned his head the feather brushed the bartender's face. Before I could lift my freshly manicured nails to wave, Mr. Dyer plucked the feather from the hat and cracked it over his knee with gratuitous force. He then threw the pieces to the floor and stepped on them as Klauss laughed darkly. I slipped past the bar and squirmed between the wall and a potted ficus near the bar entrance, and I missed most of Mr. Dyer's tirade because I was worried about being seen. If caught I could say I'd lost a contact lens while squinting to read the signature on the painting near the tree, or I could say I was near-sighted and lost my way into the bar, or I could simply say I was an interior decorator admiring the richly glossed paneling.

As I slid my back against the slick wall, I heard Mr. Dyer demand that Wilms take off what was left of the hat.

"You look like a moron," he said. "I'm so sick of you and those get-ups—the turbans, the capes, the glasses—why don't you grow up?"

"Every day is Halloween," said Klauss.

"Not anymore," yelled Mr. Dyer, "your gravy train's just derailed. Does my daughter know that you dress like the Jack of Spades? That on Fridays you pretend you're Zorro? What do you think she'll do when I tell her?"

"She already knows."

"Does she know how disgusted I am that she married you?"

"We talk about it daily," said Klauss, "and it makes her love me even more."

Mr. Dyer stormed from the bar then, barreled across the lobby and disappeared through the leather-padded front doors. Indiana Jones, after studying the broken feather in his left hand for several seconds, stumbled toward the restaurant entrance. I kept my position for a few minutes, mulling over the ramifications of this newfound information. Nobody at the firm knew Klauss was Mr. Dyer's son-in-law—he never wore a wedding band—and I wondered why it was kept secret. Shame, most likely. Mr. Dyer was embarrassed about his daughter's marriage and Klauss was willing to keep it under wraps in exchange for a free ride. Of course there was always the danger of mutiny if the senior decorators learned of Mr. Dyer's callous disregard of the company's nepotism policy, so the secret served them both.

As I squirmed from between the wall and the plant, my dress strap suddenly caught on a piece of molding and as I tugged free I lost my balance and fell forward into the tree, hugging it tightly as we crashed to the floor. I straddled the plant for what felt like minutes while trying desperately to regain my footing, and it was Lansky and DeNikers who first saw me.

"Hey, Ethel," Lansky nudged DeNikers while pointing at me, "Lucy's here."

I pulled myself up, brushed the wilted coif from my eyes and pushed through the great padded doors, not unlike Mr. Dyer had only moments before.

***

Klauss's behavior toward me remained unchanged after the La Chasse incident, and I wondered if the evil twins had told him of my ill-fated dance with the ficus. Surely he would realize I was spying on him, that it was possible I now carried a dangerous secret, the implications of which were still uncertain. But he continued to shoot at me in his offhand way, to demand I make him copies of articles from the lobby issues of *Rolling Stone*, or to ignore me altogether. When I became curious, even obsessive about his arrangement with Mr. Dyer and started spying on him at work, I learned how simple it is to watch someone who holds you in utter disregard. I was like a tolerated fly in the room; as long as I didn't land in anyone's yogurt I would not be dispatched. Before meetings I noticed that Klauss was vocal, throwing suggestions out to the senior decorators and commenting rancorously on their work. But his demeanor changed when Mr. Dyer swung open the large glass doors to the conference room and plopped into the black swivel chair at the head of the long mahogany table. He became quiet, watchful. If his colleagues regarded Klauss a little skeptically, I think they swept the notion away like so many bagel crumbs; why shouldn't they believe he had been a successful decorator on the west coast and now assumed a consulting position here? He acted the part well. He was eccentric, trendy and confident to a fault.

During meetings and work hours I watched Klauss traipse around the office in toreador pants and a matador hat, a flight jacket and goggles, Birkenstocks and knickers, and I noticed his easy friendliness with the evil twins, Lansky and DeNikers. He never worked overtime—he never worked a full week, for that matter—so when he stayed late one night this behavior blipped on my radar screen like an epileptic UFO. Of course I stayed, huddled in the corner of the small office I shared with three interns and two other "understudies," as we came to be known. When I finally stood, the pain in my cramped legs was nearly unbearable, but I remembered the ficus incident and made no sudden moves. I allowed the blood to seep back into my aching calves as my eyes adjusted to the dark. I was not worried in the least about being discovered; if anything, this type of erratic and inexplicable behavior seemed to endear designers to their superiors, provided they weren't married to the senior partner's daughter.

Stepping easily into the hallway, my footsteps muffled by the tightly woven Berber carpet, I saw a wall of light emanating from the glass-walled conference room. The thought of Klauss simply gnawing on a bagel disappointed me greatly, but I moved forward in the dark, imagining myself a frightening specter, a vengeful goddess. If nothing else, this presented the opportunity to scare the toreador pants off him. As I neared the room, I saw shadows darting off desks, walls and cabinets in the offices parallel to the conference room, and I thought he may have been exercising in there. But when I turned the corner into the hallway alongside the room and peered through the thick green glass, I saw Klauss sitting in Mr. Dyer's leather chair at the head of the mahogany table, his face buried deeply into the huge breasts of the woman who straddled him. She had dark hair, and for a moment I imagined she was Klauss's wife, that they were fulfilling some rebellious desire to fornicate in her father's power symbol. But when she threw back her head and lay it on the glossy table, her hair spread like a thick fan around her, I realized that those huge white breasts were attached to Vicky Lansky. Frozen, I watched as Klauss licked her stomach, and when she turned suddenly, her right breast knocked off his matador hat. She was facing me then, and it wasn't until she opened her eyes, smiled wickedly and yelled, "Hey, it's Lucy," that I realized I was standing too close to the glass. Lansky laughed, but the bullfighter turned white, and at that moment I did something that changed the course of my life: I stepped confidently into the conference room.

"Does Mr. Dyer know about this?" I asked. Klauss looked stricken.

"He has no problem with round-the-clock use of the conference room," Lansky grinned slyly as she drew her red silk shirt over her breasts.

"No, I mean about you two?"

"What are you talking about?" Klauss asked weakly.

"What does he care?" said Lansky, walking her toes along Klauss's bare chest until he pulled away from her and fumbled for his hat under the table. He had unwittingly handed over the power then; when he looked up at me his eyes were two white flags. I slipped through the glass doors, down the hall and into the night like a bad dream.

The next morning Klauss called me into his office. He was wearing a T-shirt with a tuxedo painted on the front and a top hat.

"Please," he said, "sit down. Would you like a bagel?"

I shook my head.

"What are you going to do?" he asked, and I was surprised by his candor.

"The questions is," I said, "what are *you* going to do?"

"What do you want?" he asked as if this was a familiar drill.

"I want you to quit treating me like your personal secretary. I want you to push for better assignments for me during meetings. I want you to get me on Lansky's cable show."

"You conniving little bitch," he said. "I won't do it, and you wanna know why? 'Cause you'll never go to Dyer. What does he care if his employees date? He'll throw you to the dogs for starting trouble, you little shit. Get the hell out."

Certainly he'd caught me off guard, and I realized instantly why Mr. Dyer hated him. I had no immediate response to his refusal, but I smirked confidently and sauntered out of his penthouse office and back to my cubbyhole. I still held the trump card: Klauss wasn't aware that I knew he was married to Dyer's daughter.

A week went by, during which Klauss appeared to be avoiding me. There were no requests for copies of articles about Fleetwood Mac's triumphant return or the sighting of Elvis Presley at a New York *Wendy's*. Klauss appeared, coincidentally, the same day I received a call from Eunice Krommer concerning an overhaul of her thirty-four room mansion in Bristol. She was so pleased with the work I'd done on her husband's business that she wanted to give the account to Dyer & Bramble with the provision that I be promoted to consultant on the project.

"I already called Mr. Dyer and insisted," she said. "He said you were only a junior partner or some such poppycock, but I stood firm. I told him he could take a lesson or two from you on customer relations. I told him I would call Mr. Bramble if I had to."

Sure enough, Dyer called me into a meeting after lunch, and the interns and understudies gave me two thumbs up as I grabbed a notebook and exited my cubicle to follow him out of our tiny office and through the heavy glass doors of the conference room. Everyone was already seated, and Klauss seemed particularly contemptuous in his Dallas Cowboys football jersey as he tapped his cleats on the white marble floor.

"First order of business is a high profile residential redesign," said Mr. Dyer. "We're looking at six figures here, and plenty of time and patience." He rubbed his temples. "DeNikers?"

"Who is it?"

"Krommer."

"The ice cream nuts?" she said, dismissing them with a wave of her hand. "God knows they'll want avocado kitchen appliances and shag carpeting. They'll make us look bad."

"We give every customer what they want," said Mr. Dyer, "especially those who want to redecorate to the tune of *six figures*." He then turned to me. "Mrs. Krommer has asked that you be, um, involved in the project?" he asked, perhaps pitying me. I realized then that Mr. Dyer didn't want to risk Eunice Krommer's call to Mr. Bramble, that I wouldn't have been there had he not planned to follow her directive. He was probably throwing bait to the other decorators before telling them they would be reporting to me, perhaps even deceiving them into believing I was already on board as a gopher, a secretary, a whipping boy. It was then that my plan came to me in its entirety.

"Mrs. Krommer already called me," I said, "and I thought Klauss, with his unique stylistic insight and understanding of the unusual, would be the perfect designer for the job."

Klauss just laughed until I said, "Maybe he could get Vicky to help him. I know they work well together."

Mr. Dyer narrowed his eyes as Klauss stared holes through me.

"What do you think, Klauss?" I said. "There might be some late night conferences, but I think you can handle *that*."

I smiled and turned to Mr. Dyer, who must have sensed I was wielding some sort of power over his opportunistic son-in-law. "Well?" I said to Klauss. "Your call."

He stared a while longer before shrugging. "I guess," he said.

Mr. Dyer, whose eyes widened, was apparently shocked that Klauss had actually accepted an assignment, and a loathsome one at that. Certainly he suspected foul play then, but didn't let on.

"All right," said Mr. Dyer as he scribbled across the dry erase board on the table before him, "Poole and Wilms on the Krommer account with Matthews as consultant."

A small gasp worked its way through the room.

"She's worked with them before," said Mr. Dyer, whose tone suggested his decision was not negotiable.

Octavio Poole, a talented but passive senior decorator, let out a small groan at the news of being saddled with the Krommers, but Klauss tilted his chair back and stared at the ceiling, perhaps wondering if Mr. Dyer and I were in league against him. Already I had visions of the entire Krommer overhaul being featured on Lansky's cable show.

We met with the Krommers the following morning, and as Klauss entered the conference room with a tray of whole-wheat bagels, Eunice Krommer let out a pained cry.

"Young man," she said, "we do not eat ice cream, and we do not eat bagels."

"Of course," said Klauss, backing slowly from the room.

When he returned she seemed to have forgotten he'd been there earlier.

"Young man," she said, "that is a fetching sombrero."

Klauss nodded, and Mr. Krommer promptly spread a blueprint of his four-story, 38,000-square-foot mansion across the table. "We're gonna tear her down, and we're gonna build 'er back up," he said, bouncing his index finger on the blueprint.

"Ah," said Klauss.

"But don't worry," added Mrs. Krommer, who mistook his dread for anxiety, "Ms. Matthews will answer all of your questions. She knows our style. She'll tell you exactly what to do."

She winked at me, and I turned to Klauss.

"I'll need several copies of that blueprint," I said offhandedly, and the disgruntled gringo smiled as he shot his finger at me, blew on the tip and shoved it into the pocket of his faded poncho.

About the author:

Dorene O'Brien is a Detroit writer whose work has earned the *Red Rock Review*'s Mark Twain Award for Short Fiction, the *New Millennium Writings* Fiction Award, the *Chicago Tribune* Nelson Algren

Award and the international Bridport Prize. She was also awarded a creative writing fellowship from the National Endowment for the Arts and her stories have been published in special Kindle editions. O'Brien's fiction and poetry have appeared in the *Connecticut Review*, The Best of *Carve Magazine*, *Short Story Review*, *Passages North*, the *Baltimore Review*, *The Republic of Letters*, the *Montreal Review*, *Detroit Noir* and others. Her short story collection, *Voices of the Lost and Found*, won the National Best Book Award in short fiction. Visit her web site at doreneobrien.com

STAMPING HIS GET
©2016 by Mike Tuohy

"Soon as I open his trailer door, I smelt smoke, like burning plastic. There's Harlan, pulling on the ceiling fan fobs trying to figure out which is the light—what's burnt out, anyhow—and which is the fan motor, what was buzzing like a June bug and not turning." Daddy paused for a slug of beer.

I turned another page in the photo album for Mama. Doctor Pelham said it might help restore her memory.

Daddy belched and picked up where he left off. "I settled that by hitting the wall switch. Motor quits buzzing. Harlan looks at me like I just cured cancer. That's when I see his fishing rod dangling, monofilament all wrapped and melted around the fan shaft. Damn fool was practicing casting inside his trailer on account of it was raining. Stupid idjit." He took another pull.

Mama didn't miss a beat. "Well, he *is* your brother."

Daddy flushed and sat up straight. "What the hell you mean by that, Nadine?"

I put out my hand. "Daddy! You know Mama had a stroke. Dr. Pelham warned us she might say inappropriate things for a while."

"Ain't no call for being sassy. She ain't too big for a whooping."

I hated when he talked so, not that he ever raised his hand against Mama. "Daddy, you know tomorrow's Sunday."

His eyebrows went up. "Thanks for reminding me, Tammy June. I need to stock up."

Mama giggled as he ran his hand under the sofa cushions where she sat. I stood up when he got to my end.

Daddy hooted when he found two quarters and a dime, then gave me a stern look as he handed me a crumpled condom foil. "Not happy you're still seeing that Bradley but I'm glad you are using protection. World don't need no more of his kind."

Having no good defense for a boy who never had money for a date but always seemed to find enough for a new tattoo, I kept quiet as Daddy finished his rounds and raided the change jar in the kitchen. He kissed Mama's forehead as if punching a clock. She stared straight ahead until the door slammed shut.

I gently shook her shoulder. "Mama! You having one of your spells?"

The roar of an un-mufflered engine signaled Daddy's departure. She blinked a few times as if coming out of a trance. "What in the world is going on?"

She looked down at the photo album. "I miss your daddy."

"He'll be back. Just went out for Sunday beer. Now who is that?"

She studied the faded image of an elegant couple in front of a drug store with signs boasting of a soda fountain and a wide variety of pomades. "That there's your Grandma Taylor. She just been proposed to. Don't she look happy?"

We were making progress. Two days before, she identified the same woman as Eleanor Roosevelt. I selected an album my sister brought over that morning, a more recent collection from our childhood. After three days of black and white and sepia, color photos seemed cheesy, though my kinfolks' fashion choices may have played a part.

Mama's face brightened at my tenth birthday party, my long hair tempting the candles on the cake. "Oh, you were such a pretty little girl in your pink party dress!"

"Yes, Mama. I remember when you picked it out." I hated that dress. Not really fond of the picture, either. Missing two front teeth might be cute. Missing one looked plain ugly.

I turned to a group shot of adults crowded around a bassinette. I recognized few faces.

Mama reeled off a string of names I hoped were right. "That's Pastor Griffin. His wife, Amelia. That one there is Mr. Sentell. He owned the hardware store. There's your daddy. This one here is Hank Venable. He worked at the gas station for years and years."

"Back up a minute, Mama. That is not Daddy. That looks more like Doctor Holt."

Mama's eyes widened. She briefly cupped her hand across her mouth. "Oh, that's what I meant." She took a deep breath. "I mean, you know, I had me a stroke and I may mix things up a little."

As she blithered on I studied the red-haired man in the photograph. Tall. Athletic. Handsome. Not at all like my daddy. I last saw him after my first period, just before he died. I remember how folks at the funeral kept glancing at me so oddly. I thought then it had to do with my budding breasts, of which I was so proud. "Wasn't Dr. Holt your obstetrician?"

Mama looked down and quickly turned the page. "We just called him the baby doctor. He made babies. I mean, brought them into this world. Let's look at some other pictures. Well, looka here! Your brother Joe's high school graduation. We wondered if he was going to make it through before he aged out."

Something about that image caught my eye. At fourteen, I stood half a foot taller than my not-so-scholarly brother, nearly twenty-one the day of his graduation. Our elder sister, Jean, even shorter, took up twice my width. Joe and Jean shared Daddy's squint and prominent incisors. The three of them had the same black hair and uniform tan Daddy claimed came from a Cherokee ancestor. My red hair, blue eyes and pale, freckled complexion made me look like an intruder. A year later, I would be a blonde with a makeup mask. No more like them and even less like me.

Mama looked straight ahead and clapped the book shut. "Ain't it time for Reverend Carlisle? Where's the remote at?"

While she flipped through the channels, I sat back and considered the implications of my mother's slip. If Doctor Holt was my father, not much to be done about it now. If it involved rape, would she have kept his photograph around? What did Daddy know about it? They had some rocky times. Maybe this had something to do with that. I struggled to imagine her mind at the time, with two kids who favored their father a little too much. As siblings, I loved Jean and Joe. As offspring, I might hesitate to have another of either.

Something about Daddy's side of the family, the Boyd clan, always troubled me. At least half-a-dozen of my Boyd cousins had criminal records. Small time stuff—shoplifting, car theft, DUI. Each story of their getting caught involved exceptional stupidity.

No geniuses on Mama's side but at least most of my Taylor cousins made it through high school. Never knew of any of them to get into much mischief. Then I remembered the July 4th picnic when my Aunt Ida, Mama's sister, threatened to beat one of her boys like 'a red-haired stepchild' after he squirted mustard on his sister at dinner. The term meant nothing to me, a nine-year-old tomboy, until the hush set in and I noticed everyone looking at me. I asked Mama what it meant and she looked from sister to sister and uncle to uncle, then to me.

"Don't mean nothing, honey. Just one of those things people say that they oughtn't."

That settled the issue for me that day. The fireworks were underway outside. Twelve years later, the term burst in my gut like a cherry bomb.

Doctor Holt's children turned out alright. His daughter became a veterinarian. I took my own collie to her for spaying. Her brothers went into law. Were they now my half-siblings? So many things I wanted to ask Mama but not in her condition. It would be cruel, maybe give her another stroke. I might have to learn to live with the mystery.

I thought about all the teasing over years about my hair; how I could not wait to be a blonde or even a brunette. I remembered Joe's embarrassment when they held him back a second time and it looked like I might catch up to him in school. How my sister got so hateful when I failed to fill her hand-me-downs, growing up instead of out. Did Mama even know what she did to me?

Reverend Carlise's topic that day came from Genesis: the story of Cain and Abel, sons of Adam and Eve. A family tree simple as a tuning fork. No question of who begat whom. One brother killed the other. The first dysfunctional family. It brought to mind the last Boyd get together. They were scrappers. I hardly noticed at the time but when I played back the picnic videotape for Mama, the soundtrack caught my ear. Parents yelling at their kids to quit trying to drown each other. Wives hollering at their husbands to back off drinking. Fathers urging their sons to stop crying and hit back. A whole lot of Cain in that bunch. I wondered if my kids would turn out so, then it hit me. I might have no Boyd blood in me. I might not be one of *those* people.

I watched Mama as she listened, transfixed, to Reverend Carlisle's sermon. She knew her Bible, especially Genesis, having started many times to read the Good Book from beginning to end. She never got through the Old Testament before having to put it aside to deal with a baby or a sick relative, doing the Lord's work instead of just reading about it. So, maybe she sinned. Lots of folk sinned. Had she not, I would not be me.

The show went to commercial, breaking the spell. Mama looked back at me. "What's the matter, Tammy June? You look worried."

I stood and stretched, feeling my face break into a grin. "Not worried about a thing, Mama. Matter of fact, I have made a decision. I am going back to school."

She put her hands together. "Praise Jesus! I've been praying for this day!"

"Well, whatever it is, I believe I have been called to go into medicine. Nursing school. Maybe medical school. We'll see how it goes."

"Oh! You would make a fine doctor. You have the genes." There went the hand over the mouth. "I mean, the smarts. You know I had a stroke."

That settled it. I was a doctor's daughter. She would know I knew when my red hair grew out. In the meantime, there would be only happy talk. "By the way, Bradley's brow ring's infected again. He spent his medicine money on another tat. I paid for the antibiotic so he wouldn't lose his face. He's already talking about getting spider webs on his neck though he can't make his car payment. I'm through with dumbasses like him."

Mama pressed her hand to her bosom and slowly nodded as our eyes met.

About the author:

Born in New Jersey in Eisenhower times, Mike moved to Georgia in 1965, witnessing much history there. A professional geologist working the environmental consulting rackets in the southeast U.S., he finds time to make friends, family and co-workers nervous as he chronicles the preposterous through short stories and novellas. He is currently working on a novel. His work has been recognized in numerous writing competitions. Fifteen of his stories, including a Pushcart nominee, have been published. A two-time finalist in *The New Yorker* Cartoon Caption Contest, he has a total of nine words in that prestigious publication

.

CAMARILLO
©2016 by Tom Stock-Hendel

"Welcome to your kingdom," said Jim, stepping into the nursery, his three-day-old son, Peter, cradled along his forearm. It was surprising how light and easy the baby fit there, his buttercream head resting on Jim's bicep globe. They had just come home from the hospital and Jim wanted to be the one to show Peter his new room. He had, after all, stayed up most of the previous night finishing it.

Up until Edie's pregnancy, the room had stood white and empty since they bought the house two years before. That had been 1949, and they and all the other postwar newlyweds gobbled up the three-bedroom homes sprouting up everywhere along freshly bulldozed and blacktopped streets.

Jim flicked on the light. "Here it is, champ." Peter's eyes, a surprising navy that the nurses had told them would probably turn brown, moved slowly beneath thick lashes, his expression mildly quizzical.

Jim introduced Peter to his crib and explained the virtues of a good night's sleep. He turned to the dresser that was stuffed with folded diapers, little white shirts and tiny socks that their friends had heaped upon them, one more in the round-robin of baby showers going on throughout the neighborhood. He showed Peter the blue wallpaper patterned with teddy bears in baseball uniforms. Three months earlier, he and Edie bought boy and girl stuff, then had to wait until the birth to find out which to use. Last night, when things at the hospital had slowed to a calm routine, Jim ran home, brought out the blue bedding and hung the wallpaper. He could still smell the paste. "Sorry about those bubbles there," he said. He pointed out the pictures on the wall of nursery rhyme characters. "Cut out special for you by your mommy from perfectly good books."

Peter looked up at his father's face.

Edie stood in the doorway, leaning on the doorframe, her body exhausted, her smile satisfied. She crossed over to the yellow rocker with the tufted blue cushion on the seat, leaned back in the chair and held out her arms for the baby. But Jim had one more thing. "Look here, Peter." He picked up a music box—the kind with the little crank that dragged a bumpy drum across the tines. The dark eyes locked on the clumsy fingers turning the little handle. Mild tinkling warmed the space.

***

Jordan pulled the visor over to the driver's side window to block the midday sun.

From the passenger seat, Peter cocked an eyebrow at him. "You remember Rod Serling?"

"Yes, I do."

"There's a signpost up ahead," Peter intoned. "Next stop."

"Very funny, Dad." Jordan tweaked the visor but hot sunlight still fell on his cheek as he drove west on the 101. "This is not a different dimension. It's only a change."

Peter stared out his window. Jordan knew he wanted to roll it down and spit, knew the pre-spit working of the jaw and curling of the lips. But after his mother had countless times called it disgusting, his father only lobbed high-speed loogies out his car window when he thought no one could see.

Jordan was driving his father to Camarillo to look at an apartment. Peter had found the place himself in the newspaper and called to set up the appointment. Not that he was unhappy in Sherman Oaks, in the heart of the San Fernando Valley. He had lived there for the entire decade since the divorce in the same two-bedroom apartment.

It was on the second floor of a beige stucco, three-story complex with twisting walkways that led to swimming pools, workout gyms and community rooms. While Peter only took a dip in one of the pools every couple of weeks during the summer, the facilities were well-used by his neighbors, most of whom were half his age or younger. If asked, Peter would say being around all that young, well-toned and tanned skin kept his blood pumping in the right direction. As far as Jordan could tell, he'd made few friends there.

Much of Peter's social life revolved around the second bedroom that he had turned into a little music studio. He staple-gunned soundproofing to the walls, got some microphones and a computer for recording, then played music a few times a month with the same two buddies he had known since Jordan was a kid. They would sit in a circle, play guitars and sing three-part harmonies. The blend of their voices took some getting used to, but Jordan had always found a rough charm to their sound and, once they had practiced a piece, they rarely missed a note. Sometimes, they'd get a gig at a small club or coffee house, and Jordan knew Peter was at his happiest walking off some little stage after a good performance. Peter had cancelled more than a few dinners with Jordan and Beth when the guys wanted to come over to his apartment to play.

But Sherman Oaks had become too expensive.

Peter adjusted an air conditioning vent. "So, how's Beth feeling?"

"Fine," said Jordan.

"Didn't she do that thing again?"

"In vitro. We decided to put it off for a while." Jordan and Beth had planned on going for another course right after the first failed, but then the real estate market tumbled and her commissions sank. They hoped to have enough money by next year.

"So how does that work?" Peter asked. "What do you have to do?"

"What do you mean?"

"Well, do they got some fancy way of doing it? Or do you just squirt into a cup?"

Jordan checked the rearview mirror. He was speeding now,

coming up on eighty miles-per-hour.

"Cup," he said. Air-conditioned cold room, green walls, fluorescent lights. At least Beth would come in to help. They wanted a good collection.

"Hey, it's got to be better than giving blood." Peter winked.

"Sure, Dad." It was his father's way of trying to make light, Jordan knew. They had talked about it before, the monthly hope and dejection, the bedroom in the condo that couldn't yet be called the baby's, the wondering about justice and who divvies out the goodies and, of course, the blame. The culprit was low sperm count. Peter had offered to take responsibility for passing that on since it had taken a few years to make Jordan, an only child. But, whatever the reason, it was Jordan's balls that were flat. And every month when Beth's period came, reliable as church bells, he had to search for a way to live with the guilt over something he couldn't change, and to somehow convince himself he wasn't a totally inadequate husband for causing the greatest disappointment in Beth's life.

Jordan drove over the crest of a hill. A valley spread out before them. Camarillo lay on one side of it—a wide, flat pancake of a town, its buildings indistinct speckles of brown and black. The other side was blanketed by low green fields. Large, spindly devices rolled through the crops like giant praying mantises, spreading the blessing of water. The freeway turned through the valley's center like a concrete river and the sky rang out over it all, a richer, clearer blue than the smog-washed paleness of the city's. They were less than an hour away from where the family had lived all of Jordan's life, but he couldn't remember his father ever coming here except maybe stopping to get gas on the way to Santa Barbara or Hearst Castle.

Peter looked down on the valley then turned back to his window and watched the side of the road go by. His hair curled over his collar, more salt than pepper. He had cut off his ponytail the year before, the ponytail he had brushed out every morning of Jordan's life. Jordan was always amazed by his father's hair, thick as a milkshake, barely thinning in the back. His forehead was high, but when you hit the sixty-two-year-old hairline, you hit a wall.

For Jordan, totally bald on top by twenty-five, it was a wonderment. But Beth liked his baldness, or that's what she said. She got him to shave his entire head, rubbed her hands over his scalp like it was a pumice stone and pointed out how he had been right at the forefront of fashion.

"Is that cactus?" Peter's glasses rose up on his nose as he squinted.

Green disks of the plant covered the ground off the side of the freeway. "Looks like," said Jordan.

"Jeez. We're not in Kansas anymore." Peter leaned his head back on the seat.

Peter could no longer find enough work in the city. For over thirty years he pulled audio cables around movie and television stages, attached microphones to lapels and necklines under some of the most famous chins in America and recorded the words for millions to hear. The work had been slowing down over the last five years or so, but now, with this latest economic mess, there were too few people around to even pick up the phone when he called.

Jordan and Peter had crunched numbers late into the night, papers spread out on Peter's brown dinette table, their asses aching on the flat wooden chairs. They shuffled expenses around, and shuffled them again, but the hard truth was that Peter was sucking out his savings way too fast. After the hit his 401K took when the market tumbled, staying in Sherman Oaks just wasn't viable. It made more sense to retire early and downsize the lifestyle. Jordan suggested Camarillo. A friend's parents raved about how happy they were there and regretted they had not moved from L.A. sooner.

"It's affordable," Jordan said, "and the senior community is supposed to be hopping."

"That's because one foot's already you-know-where," said Peter.

Jordan turned off the freeway and merged onto a six-lane street with a wide median, almost empty sidewalks and block after block of low, light-brown shopping centers. Peter stared out his window, saying nothing.

Jordan turned into the underground garage of a sprawling, pale white stucco apartment complex with red Spanish-style roof tiles.

Peter sighed.

They parked and followed signs leading them out of the garage and along a walkway towards the rental office. Unseen insects buzzed faintly.

Jordan inhaled. A touch of sweet fragrance complimented the dry warmth. "The air's clean out here."

"Squeaky," said Peter.

Peter abruptly turned off the walkway. Jordan followed him as he cut between two buildings to get to one of the pools. A handful of people lay in the loungers under umbrellas, reading or talking quietly, towels draped over their legs in the sun. Two couples played cards around a table. One woman in the pool did a careful, deliberate breast stroke, her chin raised slightly above the surface, her bathing-capped head bobbing like a volleyball in the pool's tiny chop. All were older than Peter's Sherman Oaks neighbors. Much older. Peter curled his lips but, Jordan noticed, he swallowed the spit. They turned away from the pool.

As they approached the rental office, a woman, much younger than anyone they'd yet seen, stepped out and shook their hands. Her nameplate said *Helen*. Assuming without asking that Peter was the prospective client, she aimed her pitch at him. Walking toward the available apartment at a good clip, Helen gestured with the fist-sized, jangling ring of keys in her hand, pointing out all the amenities the complex had to offer.

"Look, Dad," said Jordan, "tennis courts."

"And there's a pool table in the social room," said Helen.

Peter slowed down, letting Helen walk ahead. He put his hand on Jordan's shoulder. White stubble glinted on his cheek in the sunlight. "You can stop selling it. I'm here."

Jordan nodded.

Helen unlocked a door into a bare, white walled two-bedroom apartment that, thanks to wider windows, felt airier than Peter's Sherman Oaks place. A fireplace featured a faux-adobe brick hearth and the kitchen was brightened with Southwest-inspired colored tile.

Jordan could see that there was plenty of room for Peter's simple furniture.

Peter flipped a couple of light switches and looked inside the empty refrigerator.

"Looks like a good fit," Jordan said after checking the bathroom faucets and toilet.

"I guess so." Peter closed the sliding mirrored door to the closet in the master bedroom. "Never saw much need for a fireplace in Los Angeles."

Helen handed Peter the top sheet off a small stack of papers on the kitchen counter.

"Damn." Peter stared at it for a moment before passing it to Jordan.

The rental price was a few hundred dollars over Peter's limit. Peter had confused the numbers and thought the two-bedroom apartment was going for the rent of the one-bedroom.

Heading back to the San Fernando Valley, Peter leaned his head against the car window, the full bore of the late-afternoon sun shellacking his face.

Jordan glanced over his left shoulder to change lanes on the freeway. "The one-bedroom wasn't too bad."

Peter let loose a long, groaning sigh. "I love my second bedroom. I get the music going and I'm somewhere else. And it's the place where the guys come to play. You think they're going to drive all the way out here and we can't even record?"

"Dad, they're your friends."

Peter leaned back in his seat, staring ahead. "I should have listened to your mother. I should have gone back to school, concentrated on a real career instead of something some guy half my age can do better." He turned his gaze out the side window. Off the side of the freeway, groups of workers bent over like curled caterpillars made their way through acres of low strawberries. Beyond, sprays of water circled green fields, rainbows flickering in the misty edges.

Jordan wished he could find a place to pullover and talk to his father eye-to-eye. "You've just had some bad luck," he said. "Who hasn't? It could be a lot worse."

"Oh, yeah. If I'm lucky, I'll have another twenty years to just watch my life shrivel to a dot. At least my dad had the good sense to keel over before he hit seventy."

"There's other options." Jordan put his hand on his father's leg. "We'll figure something out."

Peter glanced down at his lap then turned to the window. Embarrassment reddened the curled tops of his ears. He patted Jordan's hand.

Driving back to his home, alone in the car, Jordan decided what to propose to Beth. Peter would live with them for a while. He could stay in the spare bedroom, the one that wasn't yet the baby's. With the in vitro postponed, it would be over a year before she was anywhere close to delivering. Peter could chip in money for food— perhaps even a little rent. He could share Jordan's home office, set up his music in there, invite the guys over. He would be able to save up enough to maybe change his situation. He might even find a steady job and not have to retire. Beth and Peter had always gotten along well and, besides, it wouldn't be permanent. A year tops. Beth would understand. Satisfied that his plan was, at least, workable, Jordan climbed the narrow stairway to the door of their condo.

As he entered, Beth stood up from the couch, her smile a soft welcome. She walked toward him slowly without a trace of the tension that sometimes tightened her shoulders. She draped her arms around his neck and kissed him. Jordan never wanted to take her kisses for granted. They were so warm, so full, so right there.

Her lips brushed the edges of his ear and she whispered, "I'm pregnant."

***

Kneeling by the rocker, Jim watched Edie get ready to nurse. She held Peter next to her breast and gently stroked the skin to the side of his mouth. The baby's lips parted and she presented her nipple. He drank, his gaze moving here and there, his face peaceful.

Edie rocked slow and steady. Welcome home, Peter, welcome

home.

Jim leaned back on top of his heels. It was complete. He had survived the years in the Pacific—first the Philippines, then Burma—and come home after those two bombs moved the world. He had Edie and the house. He had the job in the mill—the kind of job you could keep all your life. And now he had the future lying in front of him, its eyes drifting closed.

The skin on the baby's face had already lost its newborn crinkle, his sucking cheeks smooth and kissed with pink. Smooth as the new blacktop on the street outside, just beyond the freshly watered lawn.

About the author:

Tom Stock-Hendel has had stories published in *Superstition Review* and *Siren*, and holds an MFA from Antioch University-Los Angeles. He lives with his wife and son in the Southern California area.

THE MONSTER INSIDE ME
©2016 by S. Baer Lederman

There's a monster living inside me. I'm not pregnant and I don't have worms or anything, but there's definitely something living in there. I know because it keeps trying to get out. I hear it. I get these crusty patches of skin that turn red and crack and flake and the monster tells me to scratch them so I do and, Jesus Christ, does it feel good. Pure relief.

This isn't the kind of relief you feel when you put aloe vera on a sunburn, though. It's not even like when you finally get to take a pee in your own toilet after holding it in all afternoon and then getting stuck on a hot subway between some smelly stranger and the guy that's going deaf day-by-day listening to his crappy music too loud. You know, you finally get to your stop, you push and shove out of the station until you're on the street and then you rush down the sidewalk trying to look normal but at this point you have to go so bad your mouth is sour and your jaw aches and when you finally make it to your building you can't get the key in the door because your hands are shaking so bad, but finally you do and you make it up the stairs and then finally, FINALLY you can pee—in your own toilet—and you feel like you actually accomplished something. Even though it's just pee.

No, it's not like that. This relief is way more fulfilling.

It starts with a whisper. It feels like when you're walking through an alley and the wind blows a chill up your spine but you're never really sure if the chill is because of the wind or because sometimes in the wind, you can hear a voice. Just a little voice saying something breathy in, like, Italian—but you don't speak Italian so you're left wondering if you even heard a voice at all.

That's what it's like when the monster starts to whisper. It's like I feel it before I really hear it. Next thing I know I'm slowly, methodically pulling back the scabs until I just have this soft, red, hairless patch of skin. And it's so soft that in the next instant my nails are pulling that skin back and it starts getting clogged under my fingernails. But at that point I don't care because the monster's voice isn't a whisper in my skull anymore, it's coming out of my mouth, and it's saying *yes* and pretty soon my fingers are sticky with blood. And it feels like sex. It feels better than sex, my whole body trembles, my mind goes blank, I shudder, and then I bleed. And all the while the monster's borrowing my voice to say *yes*.

I guess I should've known. See, I kind of think I invited the monster in. I used to be a musician—I don't play music anymore. Actually, I don't even listen to it now. I used to do a lot of things. I used to wear lots of colors but now I only wear black. When I wore colorful clothing I played bad music. But once the patches started to appear and I was bleeding all the time, I started wearing darker and darker clothing until finally I was wearing all black all the time. And then I was playing great music.

When I played bad music I had to do the open-mic circuit. I didn't like playing in coffee shops. Playing in a coffee shop is like being the youngest sibling. You'll be telling a story and then all the sudden your sister or your dad is just talking over you. But you have something really important to say so you just keep trying to tell your story but they need an answer to the question they just asked your mom, so they're not talking but they're still not listening to you. So you talk a little louder and then the barista frowns at you and when your song is finished your dad looks up and says, "What was that?" So I didn't want to play in coffee shops anymore.

After one particularly bad night, I went home, lay down on my bed and thought to myself, "What could I do to be better? I would give anything to be better."

And another voice in my head said, "Anything?"

And I was like, "Yeah, anything!"

"Well, would you give up your body?"

And I thought, "Yeah, sure, why not?"

And the other voice said, "Promise?"

And so I said, "Yeah, really."

And the voice said, "Okay, now you're better." And I was! Fixed! Cured of my bad music. Within a few weeks I was playing so well, people started calling *me* to play places. But now I know that other voice in my head was the monster, knocking at the door to my body, asking to be let in. And I let it in.

A few months later I got my first patch of itchy skin. Didn't even notice it at first. I was out to lunch with my dad and he was actually listening to me. I was telling him about all the gigs I was getting when I heard the voice, distant at first, almost muffled like it was coming through a blown-out speaker. *Yes*, it said. And as I spoke, my fingers found the dry patch and slowly my nails began carving away.

I kept talking to my dad natural like, but beneath the *yes* I could hear laughter and that distracted me a little. As the laughter grew louder my fingers began frantically burrowing to the pulp and blood beneath. Suddenly I couldn't even speak. I had to excuse myself to the bathroom to finish making myself bleed. And as I scratched and scratched and blood began to run down my leg, the laughter crescendoed until my ears burned and my head buzzed.

A month after that, patches covered me from my ankles to my wrists. I started being very particular about my routine. Order, I figured, order will keep the monster at bay. I woke up every morning, put on oil, then the cream, and then lotioned myself twice over. On good days, when I scratched very little, I tried to remember what I did so that I could do that again forever. If I landed right foot then left foot out of bed one day when I didn't itch at all, it was right foot first from then on.

You're probably thinking, like, "Hey crazy person! Did you see a doctor?" Well not that it's any of your business, but yeah, I did see a doctor. She gave me a cream and told me to take baths with bleach to "kill the germs." But bleach doesn't kill monsters, doc.

Still, the routine seemed to help, so pretty soon everything had a routine. Locks came next. You know how sometimes you check the lock, then check it again and then maybe one more time to be safe— you know, to make sure your apartment isn't going to be robbed? Well, I check five times. But I'm not really checking. That's what I tell people, but I don't worry about being robbed. It's the precision of the bolt sliding home that I can't get enough of. It started one day as I was leaving my apartment. I turned the key. Then I turned it back. Then again. I couldn't stop. The whisper started and with each twist and snap, I tingled a little more. *Yes.* Over and over I turned it until my neighbor came out and asked if it was jammed or something, but I was just giving in to the mechanics of the beat.

The click of a light switch: at least four times. And doorknobs I turn left, left, then right—just to hear that spring load and snap back. The creak of the fridge door and its wet slap against the gasket: delicious. I started keeping time as I walked, counting each step, slapping my toes on the concrete for accent. It felt so good to give in, to let the routine takeover and find the rhythm in everything, to become the music.

As you might expect, my music kept getting better and better. Eventually it got so good that my skin was always cracked and weeping this sticky, bloody pus. I had to start wearing all black all the time—pants and long sleeves. My fans thought that was my thing, all black, but I wasn't trying to make a statement. I mean, how else was I supposed to hide the gummy residue of my music? And really, by that point playing music didn't even matter anymore.

It's like, you ever walk to the beach but you don't want to bring socks because socks are basically sand containers so you go sockless in your shoes and by the time you get there you have blisters so big and so raw you can't even get in the water? And then your mom pops them and you cry and you hate her for a second and then you hate yourself because you love her and she was just trying to help you out but it hurt even though now it feels better? That's how it got. All those things that were opposites somehow became tied up in the same moment. And that feeling spread. After a while there was no me and my skin and the monster and the music. Eventually we were all the same.

So I stopped playing music and completely devoted myself to the routine. I even made myself a schedule: on Mondays I would scratch my arms, Tuesdays were for my back (the most frustrating day *by far*), Wednesday was for my right leg, Thursday for my left, Friday was my belly, and then I spent all of Saturday and Sunday scratching my hips and butt.

Now I sort mail in an office that's a five-minute walk to the subway (about 465 steps including the subway stairs), two stops (or six times I hear the *shwick* of the subway door sliding), then another five-minutes to the office building (only 425 steps here, though), up three flights (fifty-six steps, a good number), and then I'm in the office. The mailroom is down the hall but I weave through the cubicles changing how I get there every day. Need some variation in your life, right?

I used to be a successful musician, now I'm a mail sorter. Am I a successful mail sorter? Well, you can't really be a successful mail sorter the same way you can be a successful musician because as a mail sorter you succeed by not getting fired. So success doesn't mean too much. Not like being a musician where success could mean everything under the sun except starving to death.

Sometimes people ask why I stopped playing music. They say I was going places—and maybe they're right. I never tell them about the monster, though. I just say I got sick of it. And maybe I did—or maybe I just found something I like more. I've grown to like wearing all black. I've grown to like having this thing that no one else knows about. My face is perfectly clear, handsome even, but beneath my black shirt and black pants and smart looking bowtie, I've got a secret.

And frankly, being a non-fired mail sorter works for me. Being a musician is chaotic—there's no stability to it. You can't have routines without stability. It's been almost two years with the monster living inside me and at this point, I don't mind the patches and I've come to love my routines and the bloody ecstasy. I used to think my routines were keeping the monster under control, but now I think the monster was just training me the whole time, slowly teaching me to think about it and only it and nothing else. Who knows, maybe the monster's a snake and that's why I'm so scaly. Either way, even though I tell myself I'm still fighting it, my really sick secret is: I can't wait to meet it.

About the author:

S. Baer Lederman hails from Rhode Island, but his years at University of Michigan taught him that he is a Midwesterner at heart. After completing ROTC and his Navy service, Baer has focused on writing. His fiction has appeared in *Dapper Press* and *Nebo*. He was also named a finalist in *Slippery Elm*'s 2015 Prose Contest, the *Scribes Valley* 2015 short story contest, and the *Providence Journal*'s H.P. Lovecraft short story contest. Baer is currently an MFA candidate at Roosevelt University in downtown Chicago.

THE ASHES
©2016 by Mary Smith

The little girl glanced toward the house which seemed a little hazy and dim in the distance. It was almost like those days that the clouds block the sun just before a storm, but she thought it must be grunge in her eyes. She knew she should check-in with her mom because she wasn't sure how long she had been gone from the house. *Gosh*, she thought, *how did I get out here so far anyway?* She dug in her toes and began to sprint. Puffs of dust clouded the ground where her feet hit, and her short, curly hair bobbed as she ran. She was careful to watch for animal dung and the dreaded grass burr patches. Snakes were few and far between where she was playing, but she kept an eye out for those as well. Why did it seem so late?

Suddenly she stopped, and turned to look back the way she had come. She couldn't say why, but she had that feeling she'd left something behind. All she could see was the dead summer grass, a few oak trees, and, again, that dimness obscuring any clear eye sight. However, she felt as though she should run back and find whatever it is that is lost. Perhaps something she had lain down and forgot about—she had lost more toys that way.

Then she heard a voice, faint and seemingly far away, calling her name. Turning, she looked towards home and saw that her mother was standing outside on the porch stoop. Her hand was shading her face as if from the hot sun, but she was clearly looking towards the child. Instead of shouting again the woman motioned with her other hand for the girl to come to her.

Glancing back once more, the girl whirled and raced to the house. As she got closer, she could see the shadowy outlines of her dad and brothers just inside the shade of the porch.

After what seemed like a very long time, she burst through the front gate of the yard and leapt into her mom's arms, all the while smiling past her mother's shoulder at her dad and siblings. They returned the smile but remained on the porch.

I'm home, she thought and shut her eyes to savor the moment.

***

Sylvia drove slowly and cautiously down the dirt road she had turned onto from Highway 87. She had been this route before and knew there would be bump-gates and cattle guards to deal with; not to mention the loose livestock that would carelessly wonder across the road, taking their sweet time getting to the other side. It was like they knew they owned the land and humans could darn well wait for them to saunter.

Sylvia also drove carefully because of the metal container sitting beside her on the front seat of her Yukon. It contained a semi-precious cargo—not to mention the mess it would make if it turned over. She had strapped it down with the seatbelt, but any sudden stops and the urn could go flying, scattering its contents to the point of not ever being re-gathered.

She had not wanted to make this trip since she wasn't country at all in her heart; she was a city girl through and through. But, she had promised and the request had been adamant. Sylvia's mom had wanted to have her ashes scattered at the place where she had been the happiest in her life, so she chose on this bright sunny summer day to honor her mother's last wishes. The Yukon moved slowly and comfortably over the ruts and bumps in the caliche road, its size and heavy springs making the ride smooth. The only worry Sylvia had was the narrow bump-gates. Last time she was here with her mom, she had lost a side mirror off the Yukon, and although insurance had covered, there had been a three hundred dollar co-pay.

Finally, the vehicle had passed through the last gate and Sylvia could exhale the breath she had been holding. Next was the road that wound around the cedar-packed hills before the cutoff for the old home place where Mom had been raised until she was a teen. There wasn't much chance that another vehicle would come from the other direction because so few people lived out this far. However, years of city living had taught Sylvia that when it came to other drivers, always expect something unexpected.

She finally reached the cut off to the old home place. Sylvia parked where she wasn't blocking the road leading to the empty lot. Weeds, wild grasses, and low hanging oak braches had taken over the old road. She remembered her mom's sadness many years ago when the house became unfit for living and was torn down. "I would like to have one more walkthrough before I'm gone," she had said wistfully.

Standing at the road's edge, she opened the urn and slowly tipped the ashes out. Just as the last of it fell, a small gust of wind blew some into the air, floating it toward where the house had been. Sylvia watched until it disappeared and, just as she was turning back to her car, something caught her attention. For a fraction of a second, she thought she saw a little girl staring back at her. Sylvia blinked and rubbed her eyes, and when she looked again there was no child there. *Must have been some ash that got in my eye*, she thought. She maneuvered the Yukon until she had turned around and headed back the way she had come.

Down at the end of the overgrown road a little girl was home again and all was right with both worlds.

About the author:

I am currently working in property management, but have done many other jobs over the years. I was born and raised in a small Texas town, and remain a country girl at heart, (although the girl part is long gone). I enjoy writing about my birthplace and some of the stories I have heard to which I add my own little twists. The Ashes, is a vision that I had when I went with my daughter to visit the home place in the country a few years ago. It was then I informed her that I wanted my ashes scattered there, where I was happiest as a child. Thus, the tale was born...

THE RELUCTANT SON OF A FAKE HERO
©2016 by Joe Dornich

At noon I climb out of the mouth of the Hollywood/Highland metro station just in time to see the 212 bus thunder past, and Frank's cape billow in its wake. He's striking the classic pose—chest out, hands fisted on his hips—and as much as I hate to admit it, he looks pretty good. Considering. He's kept up his physique. He's got actual muscles beneath his suit, unlike most of the losers out here in their Halloween costumes with the drawn-on pecs, and the injection-molded abs.

There are few tourists on the boulevard at this time of day, but soon a family of three stops to admire Frank. A series of photos are taken. In one, Frank wraps an arm around the wife, while flexing the other so his bicep bulges against the blue fabric of his suit. In another, Frank picks up their daughter, a chubby blonde in pink overalls. He places the girl on his shoulder, squares his jaw, and points a fist to the sky. Then the husband hands Frank some money.

I walk up as they leave.

"A dollar?" Frank says in lieu of a greeting. "I pick up their little piglet and the best they can do is a dollar. Jesus. I gotta start charging by the pound."

Then Frank balls up the money, and sticks it in the fanny pack he keeps hidden beneath his cape.

This is my father.

***

Three days ago my mom and her new husband had a baby. She and Richard thought that with the chaos of all of the visiting relatives, and the needs of the baby, my spending the summer with Frank might be best for everyone.

Everyone but me.

"What am I supposed to do with Frank all summer? What about my friends?" I asked, hoping Mom wouldn't mention the fact that I spend most nights sitting alone on the roof, watching the lights of the city. Watching the horizon of planes waiting to land at LAX. Watching life happen to everyone but me.

"You can always help your father with his latest business venture," Mom said. "That kind of experience will look good on a college application."

It will have to look good. It will have to look magnificent to distract from the screaming baby that is my 2.2 GPA.

"And what is Frank up to nowadays?" I said.

Since their divorce my father has bounced around from one hair-brained scheme to the next, usually leaving behind a trail of failed businesses and outstanding debts.

Mom winced slightly like she does when trying to think. "Oh, now, what was it that he told me? Something about Brand Management and Public Relations."

It turns out that Brand Management and Public Relations means Frank stands on Hollywood Boulevard dressed like Superman and poses for pictures with tourists for tips.

So, yeah, this should be an invaluable experience.

***

Frank zips up his fanny pack and then stares at me as if I've just materialized there with my suitcase and backpack. As if he hasn't noticed I've been standing beside him for the last thirty seconds, which is probably because he hasn't.

"How was your trip?" he says.

"A bus and a train."

Then Frank asks if I've eaten.

I tell him I could go for some lunch.

So we go to lunch.

We walk down to the Burrito Burro. Frank likes to stay on the boulevard when he's working. He says a lot of the costumed characters do. He says the further you get away from Hollywood Boulevard, the faster the context and environment break down. Suddenly, you're all alone. Suddenly, you're just some weirdo in an ill-fitting Toys "R" Us costume.

"That's how you get your ass kicked," Frank says. "Even in L.A."

The walls of the Burrito Burro are papered with pictures of their mascot. Benny. Benny the Burrito Burro. Alliteration abounds. Benny's a donkey with a burrito for a body: four legs, a head, and a tail sticking out of a tortilla tube. I'm not sure of the advertising intent, but, to me, it suggests that their burritos are made with donkey meat.

I order two tacos.

"So," Frank says in between bites of his burrito, "your mom kicked you out, huh? It's okay. I've been there."

"It's not like that," I say. "Mom's just got more than she can deal with right now."

Frank waves this off. "Your mother likes to think of herself as particular," he says. "I am the proof she is not. Besides, now you're free to join the family business."

"What?" I say.

"You're going to work with me on the boulevard."

"The hell I am."

"You can't just spend the summer sponging off me," he says.

I think: You haven't sent me so much as a birthday card in the last four years.

"I'll get a job," I say.

"Doing what?" Frank says. "Flipping burgers? Cutting some old lady's lawn? What's that gonna pay? Out here, I make upwards of two hundred a day."

"Really?" I say.

"Cash money. Tax free. We'll work as a team," Frank says. "It'll be good for both of us. Groups always make more than solos."

I stare at my tacos and think about it.

"Plus," Frank says, and a smile breaks across his face, and I know exactly where this is going. "You've got costumed experience."

What a jerk he is.

What a jerk he is to bring that up.

Last year I spent five soul-sucking weeks working for Luxury Souvenirs. I was hired to help promote their $5 Deal Daze. Basically, the plastic crap that usually went for ten dollars was marked down to five. To promote this bonanza of savings they stuck me outside of the store dressed like Lincoln. They gave me a black wool suit and a top hat. They gave me a stick-on beard that itched my face hours after I took it off. They gave me a cardboard sign with a giant five-dollar bill on it.

They also gave me a series of savings-related Lincoln-isms to memorize and recite.

People would walk by, and I'd say, "Emancipate yourself from the slavery of overpriced keepsakes."

Or, sometimes, I'd remind them that, "While A house divided against itself cannot stand, a price tag divided is a heck of a deal."

Did this sad charade have any impact on the customers? Any increase in revenue?

I don't know.

I *do* know that after eight hours in the sun, in that ridiculous outfit, with sweat pooled in my lower back, and my pride baked down to nothing, I'd fantasize about someone sneaking up behind me and shooting me in the head.

I think about Frank's offer. The last thing I need is another job standing in public dressed like an idiot. Then I think about two hundred dollars a day for the rest of the summer. That kind of cash could really improve my social standing. I think about junior prom, and how the only girl that agreed to go with me was the Snake Mother. That's not her real name. It's Meg. Sophomore year Meg found an egg in the field behind the cafeteria. She decided to keep it warm in her ample cleavage. Meg's sort of a big girl. Then one day, in the middle of Mr. Muzika's Econ lecture, the egg hatched and a snake came out. I think about the prom, and how when Meg wasn't looking, the guys from the lacrosse team would flick their tongues at me.

No.

Never again.

I tell Frank I'll do it when a black Spiderman walks in. Frank waves him over to our table.

"This is my kid," he says. "And this is Bugatti."

"Like the car," Bugatti says as we shake hands.

"Nice to meet you, Bugatti."

"Like the car," he says again.

"Nice to meet you, Bugatti like the car."

Then Bugatti says "Check it out" while swinging his leg wide and dropping his foot on the middle of our table.

I slide my tacos closer.

He's wearing red and black high-top sneakers with webbing on them. "Specially made," he says.

"Why not just wear the shoes that came with the costume?" I say.

"No good," Bugatti says. "Spidey boots got no ankle support."

Frank tells Bugatti about my decision to join him on the boulevard. He tells him that we're trying to figure out my costume.

"What about Captain America?" I say.

"Bad idea," Frank says. "There's already too many. You can't swing a dead cat down here without hitting a Captain America."

Bugatti nods in agreement.

"Plus," Frank says, "it's bad business to combine the universes."

"Pardon me," I say.

Frank goes on to explain that Captain America is from the Marvel comic book universe, while Superman is from the DC universe.

"You don't blend them," he says. "It ruins the credibility."

"*That's* what bursts the bubble?" I say. "That the fake people aren't from the same fake place? That, and not the fact that Mexican Spiderman is like fifty pounds overweight?"

Bugatti slams his fist on the table.

One of my tacos falls over.

"I hate that mutherfucker," he says.

"It may be stupid," Frank says, "but it matters to the people. That's the business. If you and I are going to work together, you gotta be DC."

"Okay, fine," I say, leaning back in my chair. "I'll be Batman."

Bugatti shakes his head side to side and groans at me.

"No good," Frank says. "It's the cowl. You want to avoid cowls and masks like they're an STD. Otherwise, come August, you'll be drowning in your own sweat."

I think back to the Lincoln beard.

"It's true," Bugatti says, holding up his Spiderman mask. "And I've got a high heat tolerance."

In the end, somehow, we settle on Aquaman. Frank says that I've already got the blonde hair. He says that my lanky and somewhat girlish physique won't be a problem, as Aquaman isn't really known for his muscles.

That stings a bit.

Frank says that I'll be the only one on the boulevard. He says that, combined with his Superman, we'll be a money-making powerhouse.

I agree.

I agree and become Aquaman.

***

With Aquaman I have a few options, stylistically speaking. There's the purple and blue camouflage outfit from the 1973 *Aquaman Adventures* television series starring Bruce Hortnutt. Unfortunately, that show was short lived. Turns out Hortnutt was something of a bunny hoarder. His neighbors complained about the smell for months. By the time Animal Protective Services kicked down the door, there was over a thousand of them, bunnies reproducing as they do. They said that the backyard, which was nothing more than a fenced-in field, was filled with them. They said that it was pink eyes and floppy ears as far as you could see. That you couldn't see a blade of grass. They said it was like some alternate universe where the Earth was made of bunnies.

When the news went public, Hortnutt killed himself.

So, I'm probably not going with that look.

There's also the rough and tumble look from Aquaman's edgy rebranding attempt in the mid-nineties. In this version, he has a golden harpoon attached to his left arm to replace the hand he lost in a piranha attack, which is pretty badass. But he's also shirtless, and sports long hair, and a wild, unkempt beard. I'm not sure I can stand shirtless in the middle of Hollywood Boulevard. People would confuse me with an emaciated hobo. Plus, I promised myself I was finished with stick-on beards.

Ultimately, I decide to go with the classic look.

On the walk back from the Burrito Burro, Frank says he has some emerald tights and gloves from a brief stint as the Green Lantern. He says the black trunks will be easy to find. For Aquaman's famous orange and gold-scaled shirt, Frank says he has an old wetsuit top I can use.

"It's not gonna be perfect," he says as we reach the metro station, "but you'll still look better than half of these clowns. And you'll have the advantage of standing beside me."

Then he reaches into his fanny pack and pulls out some keys. He says his apartment is off Sunset, just a few blocks past Fairfax. He says he'll see me later.

"Wait," I say. "You're not going to drive me?"

"No."

"That's like five miles from here," I say. "Why not?"

Frank sighs. Then he raises his palm, and makes a slow sweep of the boulevard, from the Baby Gap, all the way down to the Hollywood Museum of Squandered Innocence.

"I'm at work," he says.

***

I decide to walk. I decide that my forgoing the bus, and lugging my belongings down Sunset Boulevard will somehow punish Frank.

That he will see the error of his ways, and pull up alongside me, apologizing for being selfish, asking for forgiveness.

This is delusional. Frank has always only cared about himself.

For probably the last year of their marriage, Mom suspected he was cheating on her. Then, one day, her suspicions were confirmed when she found gum in his pubic hair. I heard them fighting through my bedroom wall. I heard Frank's futile attempts to convince Mom the gum was his. How it must have fallen out of his mouth and become stuck there.

"Like, maybe, when I was in the shower," he said.

There was more, but I piled the pillows over my head. I didn't want to hear. The next morning Frank was gone. Mom said he'd be away for a while, out of town on business. She said it to spare me the pain, I guess. I guess she assumed I hadn't heard them fighting. As with Frank, as with a lot of things in life, Mom gave the thickness of our walls more credit than they deserved.

A few days later I saw Frank on the high school baseball field. He was drunk, and making languid loops in the outfield on a girl's bicycle. He'd been sleeping in the dugout.

***

Frank's apartment building is one of those white stucco jobs that crumble into pebbles and powder when touched. He's got one of the ground-floor apartments, the one closest to the road. Inside it's just one giant room. Fantastic. There's a weight bench in one corner with a pair of underwear hanging off one end of the barbell. Dumbbells of various sizes and weight litter the floor. I watch my step. I head to the galley kitchen hoping for a glass of water. Tubs of protein powder and beer cans crowd the counter. Frank has exactly one glass, and there's a cigarette butt floating in it, and lipstick on the rim. I drop my pack and flop down on Frank's bed. On his nightstand are a copy of *The Entrepreneur in You*, and a framed photo of Christopher Reeve, the actor who starred in the original *Superman* movies. There's not a picture of me in sight.

I think about calling my mom. I think that if I explained the situation, Frank's ridiculous "job," and the squalor of his apartment, that she'd let me come home. Then I think she'd just as likely tell me to give it some time. To give Frank a chance and make the best of it.

I close my eyes.

The drone of the traffic is familiar and soothing.

I fall asleep.

***

I wake up to Frank kicking my foot. He's shirtless and wearing clear, plastic gloves that are streaked with black.

"Are you dyeing your hair?" I say.

"You bet your ass I am."

"Why?"

"Because you can't have a graying Superman."

"Why?"

"For the same reason Jesus died in his prime. Nobody wants to see their heroes age. It reminds them of their own mortality."

Then he waves a gloved hand at his bed and me.

"I hope you enjoyed your little nap," he says. "But don't make a habit of it."

He points to a sagging purple loveseat whose integrity looks suspect.

"That's you," he says.

"Excuse me?"

"It doesn't look like much, but it's pretty comfortable," Frank says. "And it pulls out, which makes it smarter than me." Then Frank lets out a single burst of laughter and kicks me again. Then he peels the gloves off with his teeth, and picks up a white, linen shirt from the floor. On the back of the shirt is a hula dancer with a pair of monstrous breasts crammed into a coconut bra. She has a grass skirt made of green fringe that sways back and forth when Frank moves. She is naked underneath, and rendered anatomically correct. The level of detail is alarming.

"This stuff needs fifteen minutes to set in and do its thing," Frank says, walking to the fridge. He tosses me a beer. "While we wait, let's go on the roof," he says. "It's a good place to drink, but then again most places are."

So we go to the roof.

We make our way across the tarpaper, and past all of the satellite TV dishes, to the far corner. From here I can see the traffic crawling along Sunset Boulevard. I can see how the brake lights waiver in the exhaust.

Across the street, and above the Chinese Food & Donuts place, is a billboard. They are, apparently, remaking *Citizen Kane*. The billboard features the bloated face of the Scottish actor who will play Kane. He used to be leaner, and more of a star, but lately he's only made headlines for throwing people through barroom windows, and becoming a casual anti-Semite.

Frank sees the billboard too. "Can you believe they're rehashing that garbage?" he says.

No, I think, *I can't*. Who needs another movie about someone so desperate to relive his childhood? Another movie that glorifies that time, instead of depicting it for the parade of regret and loneliness that it really is.

It's surprising to find myself agreeing with Frank. Surprising, but nice.

"I mean," he says, "when is Hollywood gonna stop pushing their homoerotic agenda?"

"Wait. What?"

"That movie's about gay sex."

"How do you figure?"

Frank holds up his hand. He curls his index finger along his thumb.

"I don't know what that means," I say.

"It's an asshole."

"And?"

"Rosebud is slang for asshole," Frank says. "The guy spends the entire movie looking for his rosebud. He's trying to relive his first homosexual experience. The movie's about gay sex."

"It's not," I say. "It's about a sad, rich guy pining for his childhood. Rosebud was the name of his sled."

"Believe what you want. But you're wrong. Plus," Frank says, "Charles Foster Kane? That's one of the biggest puffer names I've ever heard."

Then Frank belches and turns his back on me, concluding, sadly, one of our better father-son talks.

Some nights I lie awake, thinking about how half of my genetic makeup comes from this guy. Then I think about the traits I got from Mom, and I wonder if they're good enough, strong enough, to counteract Frank's contaminated contribution.

A gust of wind comes in from the west. It blows the hula dancer's skirt to the side, and I try not to stare.

I try, and I fail.

The next morning we go to work.

***

Frank insists on being on the boulevard no later than 9 a.m. Any later than that he says, and all of the quality real estate is taken. So, at 8:58 we're standing at the base of the stairs leading to the Hollywood & Highland Shopping Center.

"This way," he tells me, "we'll get all of the shopper traffic, and all of the boulevard traffic."

It sounds smart. It sounds smart until the first hour ticks by without anyone wanting a picture. No one wants a picture the next hour, or the hour after that. The only highlight of the morning is when a woman walks by with a rattlesnake tattooed on her legs. She has the snake's head on her left calf, and its body going up the back of her leg until it disappears beneath her black, leather skirt. The rest of its body continues down her other thigh, with the rattler on her right calf.

"Will you look at that," Frank says. "I'll bet the rest of that thing," and then he pauses, sticks up a finger, and makes little circles, "is coiled on her ass. Just imagine that."

Then Frank digs a small notebook out of his fanny pack and writes something down.

"What are you doing?" I say.

"I don't want to lose that," he says. "That's some beautiful imagery. It'll work great in one of my poems."

"Your what?"

"My poems. My poetry. I write poems from time to time," he says.

This is a curious development. Frank never struck me as the literary type. He used to read *Sports Illustrated* on the toilet, occupying our sole bathroom for up to an hour, but that was about it.

"I'd like to read something sometime," I say.

"Yeah, maybe," he says.

Then we go to lunch.

***

When we get back, the spot by the stairs is filled with sunshine, so we move down the boulevard and stand in the shade of the double-decker Star Sightings tour bus.

No one wants a picture.

"Let's try splitting up," Frank says. "If one of us gets a nibble, he'll wave over the other one. We'll divide and conquer."

"Frank," I say, "this is stupid. I feel stupid."

"Hey, if it was easy, anyone would be doing it. You gotta get out there and generate interest. Try using that thing you made."

The night before, Frank told me I should add a prop to my costume. Something for tourists to pose with. Something to help draw them to it.

"Zorro's got a sword," he said. "Thor has a hammer. All the lesser heroes do it."

I didn't appreciate being referred to as a "lesser hero," but then I pictured myself in green tights, and an orange neoprene shirt, and I figured I could use all of the help I could get. I spent the night taping paper towel tubes together, and covering the whole thing in aluminum foil.

It's supposed to be a trident.

It looks like a big, limp fork.

Another hour goes by. No one wants my picture. Then I see Frank pose with a young Swedish couple. A few minutes later, he takes a picture with a group of girls in matching softball uniforms.

I storm down the street.

"What the hell?"

"What?" Frank says.

"You said you'd wave me over."

"I tried," Frank says. "They didn't want their picture with you. They thought you were some kind of gay farmer."

I feel my face bloom hot with embarrassment.

I toss the trident.

I spend the rest of the afternoon across the street, sulking inside The Dripping Bean, and nursing a black coffee.

Around three, Frank comes by. He says he's going to a Happy Hour with Bugatti, and two guys who dress as Iron Man. I ask if I can come.

"You can if you've got any money," he says.

I go back to Frank's. This time I take the bus.

***

By ten o'clock Frank hasn't come home, so I steal two of his beers and go to the roof. There are never many visible stars in LA's night sky, but down here it's even worse. The streetlights, and spotlights, and digital billboards, and winking neon are too much for even the brightest of celestial bodies. The light pollution reflects off of the smog, making a gray blanket of the sky. It's easy to imagine that this is all there is. That nothing larger or grander exists beyond this tiny bubble. It's easy to imagine that we are all alone.

I walk to the edge of the roof. I have never looked over a roof I haven't imagined myself jumping off of. Sometimes I imagine the things that would cycle through my head on the way down. If there would be some clarity before I hit, and if it's better to experience that, and then have it immediately taken away, than to never have any at all.

On the other side of Frank's building is an alley. The far wall is lined with Dumpsters, and on every single one is a sign that reads: NO BABIES.

The next morning Frank wakes me with a coffee and a blueberry scone. I don't know if this is his way for apologizing for yesterday, but I'll take it.

When we get to the boulevard he hands me a folded piece of paper. I open it, and see that it is titled: *The Sex With You.*

"What the hell is this?" I say.

"My words," he says.

"What?"

"You said you wanted to read some of my stuff," Frank says. "This is one of my poems."

"Oh, okay," I say. "Sure."

I read Frank's poem.

> *The sex with you*
> *It has been terrible for years.*
> *Your vagina has become*
> *nothing more than*
> *a hole.*
> *A grave*
> *where I bury*
> *the best part*
> *of myself.*

"That's something," I say, handing that paper back to Frank. "Very evocative."

"I wrote it about your mother," he says.

"Jesus Christ! What the hell is your problem, Frank?"

"You know," he says, "you should try calling me Dad."

"Please," I say. "I'd sooner call you Superman."

***

The rest of the morning is awkward. A few people stop for pictures, but they only want Frank. Sometimes I get thrown in at the end, as an afterthought, but mostly I work the camera.

Then an Asian grandmother, with a group of kids in tow, gets my hopes up. As her grandchildren gather around Frank, flexing their little muscles, she pushes her camera into my chest.

"Pictureman," she says, smiling.

"No," I say. "Aquaman. I'm a hero too."

"Pictureman," she says again, frowning, and pressing the camera harder. Then she joins her grandchildren, everyone posing and smiling for a picture.

So I take their picture.

She hands Frank some money before they continue down the boulevard.

"Don't worry, Pictureman," Frank says. "You'll get your cut."

"This is stupid," I say. "It isn't working. I can't do this."

"Sure you can," Frank says, putting a hand on my shoulder.

"No," I say, sliding away from his touch. "I can't. I'm not like you." And as the words leave my mouth, I realize that it's true, I'm not like Frank, and that, somehow, is part of my problem.

"So, what then?" Frank says. "You want to quit? You want to go home?"

"Yes!" That's exactly what I want. Maybe if I possessed Frank's charm, or strength, or whatever it is that gives him a natural ease with people, then things would be different. But I don't. Maybe if I did, I wouldn't be cast out of my own home, supplanted by a baby my mother barely knows. Maybe I wouldn't be equally embarrassed and grateful to have the Snake Mother as a prom date. Maybe I wouldn't spend every night on the roof, alone, wishing for things to be different, and having no idea what that difference looks like.

Frank just stands there and furrows his brow. It makes his Superman curl, the one he molds each morning, then lacquers with hairspray, move ever so slightly.

"What did you say?"

"I said I'll stay," I mumble, not meeting his eyes. I shuffle to the center of the boulevard, positioning myself between the streams of tourist traffic. "I'll try."

And I do. I make eye contact. I wave. I stretch my face into an unnatural smile, and project a confidence I do not own. I make a true and unguarded attempt to engage.

No one wants my picture.

About the author:

Joe Dornich is a PhD candidate in Texas Tech's creative writing program, where he also serves as Managing Editor for *Iron Horse Literary Review*. Joe's work has won contests with SCMLA, *Master's Review*, and *Fresher Writing*. In addition to writing, Joe is also taking a mail-order course in veterinary medicine. His mailbox is often filled with sick kittens...

EMER RALD'S JEWEL
©2016 by Robin Hostetter

The wave rolled Emer over and over, each slam onto the pebbled ground dislodging more of his held breath. *Where are my parents?* The water swept him toward the tree break at the edge of town. *Why didn't the village mage stop the tsunami?* Tree branches slapped his face; he hung onto the slippery ends with desperate fingers.

The wave released him.

Emer sucked in lungsful of air and his head cleared. Roiling water covered the rocky beach that pinched his home town of Oceanside between the sea and the coastal cliffs. The roar of the water diminished and he heard screams and oaths from the water-logged town. He stunk of dead fish.

He saw the flickering of magic shields over the stone cottages of the village, their power distorting the air like mirages. The efforts were too little, too late. Emer wished he had magic to add to the defense of the town but he was only eleven years old and could not expect his magic to flower for several more years.

Emer's parents had been running beside him when the wave knocked them over, but he could see no sign of them now. Though there hadn't been a tsunami since before he was born, he knew that water that flowed in always flowed back out. Emer studied the seething waters that covered the beach. He should stay in the tree, but desperation to find his parents proved stronger.

He let go of the branches and trudged inland, the water above his knees. Within five steps, the water surged against him on its return to the sea. His feet swept from beneath him and he spluttered out his last breath into the burning foam.

Something wooden and buoyant knocked hard against him. A small dingy, torn from its mooring, trailing a frayed line. Emer, choking out stinging saltwater, clung to the gunwale as the craft picked up speed, rushing out to sea.

It took Emer five tries to clamber aboard and by then he was in deep water far off shore. Emer's father, Rald, was a fisherman and had taken Emer on his ketch many times. That was a vessel with sails and oars, and a small crew, to challenge the deep fishing beds. The dingy didn't even have a paddle.

He watched the distant shore slide by on the port side. An ocean current had his boat in a firm grip and swept him toward Scat Rocks, leagues to the south. *Towards the war.*

Emer lay back against the rough planking, folded arms pillowing his head while he stared at the sky. His salt-encrusted clothes chafed and his skin parched in the broiling sun. *Are my parents safe? They must be worried about me.* Emer choked back a sob when he thought of them searching the empty beach without finding a sign of him. Seagulls screeched overhead and wavelets lapped against the sides of his dingy.

He wondered what brought the tsunami to suddenly crash against his little village. Had the war crept up the coast in a naval battle beyond the western horizon? Did Benderbeck's mages battle old King Orrey's ships, flinging water elementals at one another?

Were the Illithids, the Deep's most feared monsters, brewing up new devilry? Was one of the bulbous-headed, tentacle-faced otherworldly mystics watching him now while cruising with its arcane powers just below the surface?

He whistled a tune to drive away the scary thoughts. Though Emer had seen magic manifest in many forms, music was his favorite. Maybe when he was older, he could put real magic into his music. Become a Harper. It was said their soaring notes made people fly. He peeked over the gunwale; until then he'd have to swim.

Emer calculated that if luck was with him, he would run aground on Scat Rocks. If a little less so, at least drift close enough to swim to the isolated black rocks and their slippery covering of white bird droppings.

Or luck might be entirely against him and he'd drift by the rocky refuge completely out of range. How far dared he swim in the dark waters? What creatures watched for him to try? As if in answer, he spotted a tall black fin cutting through the water to starboard.

Another and then another. Orcas raced him to Scat Rocks. They bolted through the waves like jack-rabbits; he floated, slow as a tortoise.

Panic parched Emer's throat. Thirst burned him.

The current took him farther out to sea; the shore now a distant line.

Beneath the waves, a grey shape larger than his father's vessel passed near the boat.

Too dry to whistle, he sang to drive away his fear. He knew many songs which the fisherman sang as they worked the ketches. Songs of gluts of fishes pulled from the water, of the defeat of the sea. Emer feared to sing those for now the sea held him captive and the fish listened.

He sang a lullaby in memory of his mother.

"Rock, rock, rock
In my arms you rock
On a gentle sea
Rock, rock, rock
Family is a rock
It your anchor be."

At first the words crawled from his scratchy throat, but as he let the message wash through him, his voice grew in strength.

"Rock, rock, rock," he sang to the sea.

The waves slapped at his dingy, rocking it in rhythm to the music.

"If you dash upon the rock
Come always home to me."

Louder and louder Emer sang and strength stirred within him.

Always before, the music magic had been a distant thing of which he'd caught the merest whisper in someone else's song. This time the power shouted within him. He was too young for such a thing and couldn't control it. The half-formed thought, more a plea to rejoin his mother than a spell of rescue, tumbled away.

Defeated, Emer ceased his singing. The sun on the waves dazzled his eyes. In one such flash he thought he saw his mother holding her arms out to welcome him. Fear fled.

He stood in the boat. "I be ready, Momma. Take me home."

A humpback whale slammed into the back of the dingy and knocked Emer off his feet. The grey leviathan pushed the boat and a creamy wake curled around the wooden sides.

White-knuckled, Emer gripped the gunwales where he had fallen, eyes squeezed shut. He wasn't afraid the whale would eat him, but feared the beast would flip the boat in playful enthusiasm. What chance did his flimsy craft have against the great bulk of the gentle giant? He hoped that the creature knew Emer's family had never hunted whales.

Opening his eyes, Emer ventured a peek forward. Wind, laced with a salty spray, slapped his face. The shore was no longer a distant line; he could make out the sea cliffs with waves breaking at their feet.

The leviathan pushed him closer to the shore and now Emer discerned figures on the sand. He heard screams and the clash of steel on steel until all sounds were drowned by the pounding of red surf.

When a tidal surge lifted the dingy, the whale gave the boat a final shove. White spray and blue sound filled Emer's world. His boat shuddered as its keel bit into the pebbled beach.

Emer cowered in the boat and gaped at the bloodied men fighting around him. A severed arm spun in lazy circles in the water, pursued by crabs and gulls alike. The salty smell of blood and sea filled his nose.

A pile-driver of ensorcelled air blasted the wooden craft and knocked Emer senseless.

***

Emer's senses returned. He lay outside a tent, shackled to a tent pole driven into the rocky ground above the tide line. The sun touched the western horizon. Smokey fires dotted the beach. Men, crabs, and gulls picked over corpses.

His tongue was sour leather and parched. The smell of vomit and shit gagged hm.

Waves broke in rhythmic rumbles counterpointed by bird screech.

A boot prodded him. "So yer awake."

Looking up at the mail-clad and bearded man staring down at him, Emer croaked, "Who you be? Where am I?" He sat up.

"I'll be askin' the questions." The man handed Emer a bowl of water and laid his gauntleted hand on a black-hilted dagger as Emer drank. The man's eyes squinted in suspicion until Emer had finished the last drop.

"What kind of water mage are ya then?" the soldier asked.

"Why, no kind at all," Emer said. "I be only eleven years. I be no mage."

"Bah," the man spat. "You may have the guise of a little boy, but you come chargin' the beach in a boat pushed by a whale familiar. You're a mage sure enough."

Emer tried to stand, but the chain shackles prevented it. "I be Emer, son of Rald of Oceanstide. Send for my father if ye don't believe me."

"Oh, we'll get proof soon enough," his captor said, "when the Blue Lady questions ya."

Emer sank down and stared at the sea. Mention of his father reminded him of the tsunami and fears that his parents were dead. A man in a blood-soaked leather jerkin and carrying a broad curved knife walked past him and stepped into the tent.

Someone inside the tent shrieked in agony, but whether the knife that wrenched the scream was held by healer or torturer Emer could not say.

The sun dropped below the horizon and the light faded. The sky still shone with a silvery sheen for the moon was swollen past three quarters.

The pebbly beach made a poor bed and Emer tossed and turned and waited. If he slipped his bonds he could follow the beach home though he would have to steal through the camp of hostile soldiers. The alternative was to forgo the straight trip and climb up the shadowy sea cliffs.

He tested the shackle's lock. If he were a Harper, the lock would be no difficulty. Harpers had the skill of thieves in picking locks. It was all about the nimbleness of fingers, after all.

Emer sighed, dropped the lock, and looked up the beach to the north. He should stop dreaming, he would never be Emer the Harper, but Emer Rald, a fisherman like his father.

A slap to the back of his head broke his reverie.

"C'mon you. Git up." The bearded soldier said. "Yer wanted in the tent."

The man unlocked the shackles and jerked Emer to his feet. He tied Emer's hands behind him and shoved the boy toward the tent opening. "Let's see how long yer keep your current glamour, little boy. Have fun, mage."

Tripod braziers illuminated the interior and Emer saw both a wooden rack and a cushioned divan. A round table in the center of the silken enclosure held a wine decanter, a bowl of stew, a bottle of wine, and an assortment of pinchers and knives. The floor was bare ground, the walls green and white striped. And smeared with blood, purple in the fire's light.

A corpse lay in one corner.

The man wearing the blood-soaked leather jerkin stood to one side, looking at Emer with a falcon's hooded eyes.

Emer felt a knife at his back and tensed.

The knife sawed through the ropes binding his hands.

"Let me have a look at you," said a feminine voice behind him. Strong fingers gripped his shoulder and turned him about. "I'm told you're a mage."

Emer faced the speaker, a tall willowy woman dressed in blue silk robes. Her face was an unnatural white—the white of dead bone. Her irises glinted the blue of deep water. Hair, dark brown and shot through with blue strands, hung to her waist.

She held him with a firm grip on both shoulders and stared into his face. "You're no mage. You're just a little boy."

Relief flooded through him. Now that it was plain he was no threat, the soldiers would help him home, or at least send him on his way.

The Blue Lady smiled and a chill ran through Emer's bones. "How marvelous." She turned to the falcon-eyed man and nodded toward the rack. "Secure him."

Terror rose to choke Emer, and he fainted when the man seized him.

A cold splash of water roused him. He was bound hand and foot to the rack, stretched just enough that he couldn't move but not so much as brought pain. The Blue Lady sat at the table, her chin leaning on her cupped hand, and stared at him.

"I said you were not a mage, but there is magic about you. Were your parents druids perhaps?"

"My father is a fisherman," Emer forced the words past dry lips.

The Blue Lady shook her head. "No, it's something else. There's something raw here." She closed her eyes and looked to swoon. "Delicious."

Emer's heart hammered in his chest; he squeezed his eyes shut to fight the tears. "Rock, rock, rock," he sang *sotto voce*.

The Blue Lady's eyes popped open. "There it is. How wonderful, how sweet."

Fiery fingers seemed to tear at Emer's throat when the Blue Lady smiled. He wanted to scream in pain, but no sound could escape.

She stood. "I shall feast on you for days. Now, sing for me."

Emer's throat was raw and he shook his head. "Can't, throat hurts."

"If you sing, I won't have to tear at you so much," the Blue Lady said. "I'll give you a moment to repair, and then we'll start again." She sipped some wine.

She walked to the tent opening and gazed out. Then she turned to the man with the blood-stained jerkin. "Leave us. See that we are not disturbed."

When the man left, the Blue Lady turned back to Emer. "Ready to begin?"

Emer shook his head, eyes closed. "Hurts."

"Oh, but pain is such a motivator," the lady said. "I'll show you." She gave the rack a small turn. "Now sing."

Pain at ankles and wrists snapped Emer's eyes open. He sang, "Rock, rock, rock, family is a rock, it my anchor be."

Strength surged within him at the words and a little of its power leaked from him. Then the Blue Lady, with a great indrawn breath, gobbled it all.

This left Emer feeling empty, and somewhat smaller, like a little bit of himself had been lost. He passed out.

Stinging slaps on his face woke him. "Again," the Blue lady said. "Sing again." She moved toward the rack's control wheel.

Emer sang before she got there. "Rock, rock, rock, if you dash upon the rock come always home to me."

This time the power surged more quickly and took the lady by surprise, for more of it got away before the Lady drank the rest.

Drained again, Emer barely held onto consciousness.

"Oh, I do so love them young," the lady said. "Before their bodies change from children. The magic is so sweet, untainted by baser things." She turned her attention to Emer. "Sleep, little one that your vessel may refill. Take an hour's respite. I shall return."

The lady swept out of the tent in a gale of blue silk and white flesh.

The Blue Lady had shown Emer that his song connected him to a fount of magic and he felt both immature and very grown up. He needed instruction on how to work the magic once summoned but knew he could not stay for additional lessons. The woman was eating him.

He tried to sing up the magic once more, but hadn't the strength.

A man, sporting no armor but wearing a cloak patched in all the colors of the rainbow, entered the tent. He strode over to the rack and leaned closer to examine Emer.

"Still alive, thank the gods. I heard the blue bitch had a new plaything. We can't allow that."

The man drew a dagger from beneath his cloak and reached for Emer's throat.

"Don't say anything, or you'll draw her back." The man cut Emer's bonds and lifted him to his feet. "Come with me, quickly. And remember, do not talk."

The man led him out of the tent. The guard in the leather jerkin slumped on the ground, snoring. "The spell will hold him a little longer if you're quiet," Emer's rescuer whispered. "Mind your step." With a finger to his lips, the man took Emer into the shadows near the cliffs that rose like a wall from the beach.

Emer followed him to the outskirts of the camp and into a wagon whose decorated sides proclaimed it the property of Leveraux's Balladeers. Inside, the man opened a crawl space under the floorboards.

"Hide in here. Say nothing. I can't emphasis that enough. The blue witch can sense your magic and will take you again. Next time there will be no possibility of rescue and she will eat your magic until you are nothing but a dry husk."

Emer wanted to say that he had no magic, but the man clapped his hand over his mouth.

"Do not speak!" The man sighed. "My name is Leveraux. My little troupe of camp followers has been entertaining King Orrey's troops. We'll break camp in the morning. Say nothing until we are well away. Plenty of time for questions later."

Leveraux repacked the floorboards above Emer. "And especially, no singing. Get some sleep."

Later, the jouncing of the wagon woke Emer. Slashes of light marked the edges of the wooden boards of his hiding place.

The wagon jerked to a stop. A gruff voice asked, "Where are you going?"

"For supplies," Leveraux answered. "We'll be back tonight."

"The whole troupe? All three wagons?"

"Not safe to travel alone. The war."

"Got orders to search all wagons. Pull up over there."

The wagon moved a short distance and stopped. The bed rocked as someone clambered aboard. Emer heard the sliding hiss of chain mail. Heavy footsteps marked the guard as he stomped around and the thump of wood on wood testified where the contents of the wagon were thrown about.

An impulse to sing erupted in Emer's mind, a command from a driving will. His defenses crumpled, sand before a hot wind.

Leveraux planted a stool directly above Emer's hiding place and sat on it. "What are you looking for?" Leveraux asked.

The alien will contending against Emer vanished. He heard Leveraux shift on the stool above him.

"Never mind," the gruff voice said. "You're clear. Move on."

The wagon started moving almost immediately. After the noises of the soldiers' camp faded behind them, Leveraux pulled open the hidden compartment and lifted Emer out.

"You did well, lad. You kept very quiet."

"I knew not to sing, but some power tried to force me."

"The mind of the Blue Lady willing you to give yourself away. I blocked it."

"Be you a mage?" Emer asked.

"No. I am a Harper."

Disbelief chased joy across Emer's thoughts. "Why did you help me?"

"You have the makings of a Harper yourself. I thought you should get the chance."

"Me? A Harper? How can that be?"

"You have the music magic. I might have missed it except for the Blue Lady's probings. But you'll need training and protection until you master your talent. Join my troupe and you'll get these things."

Emer's knees weakened as realization of his good fortune sunk in and he grabbed for the nearby stool. His dream, laid in front of him. *My parents won't believe it.*

The thought shocked all joy from his mind. Were his parents dead? Or searching for him, bereft of all hope? He had to know. He had to let them know.

"I have wanted to be a Harper as long as I can remember," Emer said. "But first I must find my parents."

Leveraux shook his head. "It's too dangerous. That blue witch knows you come from Oceanstide and is headed there now. My troupe turns aside when we strike the inland road ahead. The danger will pass in a month or two. You can look for your parents then."

Emer sat on the stool and agonized over choosing to find his mother and father at the cost of his chance to go with the Harpers, or pursuing his life dream at the cost of the peace-of-mind of both himself and his parents. His heart see-sawed on a knife's edge. Until the wagon made a right turn. A smooth grade pierced the sea cliffs here, rising inland between two high rocky shoulders.

Emer closed his eyes to hide his tears and jumped from the back of the wagon. After a longing look at the departing troupe, he followed the beach north.

Oceanstide still stood. Blackish discoloration of the first three feet of stone courses in the buildings gave the town a mismatched look. Tree limbs and broken bedsteads littered the street. People prodded among the ruined goods with wide-eyed, distant stares. The foul odor of disaster rose to meet squabbling gulls that dove at bits of drying flesh.

A row of canvas-covered bodies lay near the church.

Emer scanned the crowd of milling people, looking for two familiar figures. He didn't see them and the longer he looked the more he feared the row of shrouds at the church's door.

"Rock, rock, rock, if you dash upon the rock come always home to me," Emer sang. He called to his parents in his song, willing them to step from the stone chapel.

The church door opened.

The Blue Lady stepped out.

She saw Emer and laughed. "Foolish boy. You should have run when you had the chance. Now you're mine." She spread her arms wide.

A compulsion, stronger than the one he had felt in the wagon, called him to go to her. His feet moved in plodding steps toward the church and she walked toward him. He struggled to block the evil will from his mind but he was no Leveraux. Emer feared to sing, thinking that the urge to do so was part of the Blue Lady's spell.

The music magic crescendoed within him until he could contain it no longer. It burst forth and he sang, "Rock, rock, rock. My family is a rock. It my anchor be."

The Blue Lady shrieked. "You impudent pup. You dare defy—" She looked down in astonishment.

A shroud-wrapped arm held her ankle. Beside her, another corpse rose to its feet, hands stretching for her neck.

The witch wailed as they pulled her down.

The alien will in his mind disappeared like the dark at the striking of a match.

When the carnage was over, the two shrouded figures returned to their spot in the row of the dead.

Emer walked to them. He stepped around a pile of fleshy ribbons that clung to a torn blue dress and white bone. He nudged the carcass aside. The gulls covered it and one screeched in triumph as it soared skyward with an eyeball the color of deep water.

Emer lifted the canvas from one of the figures to gaze upon her face. "Mother," he said, voice cracking.

His tears soaked the canvas. He cried for his mother. Already he missed his father. And he'd missed a chance with the Harpers.

He sang through a raw throat. "Rock, rock, rock, in my arms you rock, on a gentle sea."

"That's a jewel of a voice you have."

Emer turned to find Leveraux standing a few feet away with his arms folded across his chest.

"I am sorry about your parents. Will you honor them, stay in Oceanstide, and become a fisherman?"

"I may wish to return some day but there is nothing for me here now."

"You are still welcome to join us," the Harper said. "At least until your voice changes."

About the author:

Robin Hostetter lives in San Antonio where he works as a psychiatrist using the new media of telemedicine. He is a retired Army colonel and full time writer. A member of the San Antonio Writer's Guild, he has authored three novels which await discovery.

CONTINUUM
©2016 by Catharine Leggett

The shoulders hunch, the broad suspender straps bunch the plaid shirt, the long slope of his back as he leans towards the window. As if he's watching an event unfold out on the sidewalk, or is about to leap from his chair; he isn't doing either. He sits. He watches. All day. Every day.

Eleanor carries the cake across the room until she stands next to him, taps him lightly on the shoulder. "Top of the afternoon, Shane." A joke, since he claims to have about as much Irish blood as a soda biscuit.

Shane smiles his wide, welcoming smile and asks, "Time for you already?" as if her appearance is a complete surprise, even though she comes here every Sunday and Wednesday at this same time.

Eleanor puts the cake down on an end table and hears Barb's mother shouting about something across the hall. Poor Barb. She is being punished by her mother for being ten minutes late. Barb had to get her three grandkids ready to be picked up by their parents, after their weekend sleepover. "Total chaos," she told Eleanor. "Herding cats. And on no sleep. But we had fun!"

Eleanor would love sleepless nights on account of grandchildren.

Shane's eyes are on the cake and his hands plunge from the armrests to his lap, his shoulders sink down even deeper. "Oh my," is all he manages.

"What do you think?" Eleanor asks. "Amazing, right?" She pulls a chair up beside him. "It was a challenge, I can tell you."

His chin quivers, and he shakes his head.

"It's a daffodil cake. I made it especially for you. After hearing your story, the one you told me the other day." She waits for him to say how beautiful it looks, or how delicious, then follows his gaze to the street, to the flow of people on the sidewalk, and to the sky as a tiny, silver dart, silent and dazzling under the bright sun, pierces the blue.

"Cat got your tongue today?" She can always count on him to toss out a quick retort.

"I didn't tell you the whole story." A catch in his voice chokes him.

Across the hall, Barb's mother shouts. What now? Something about someone stealing her clothes. Once again she is the victim of some injustice. Barb will never be able to make her happy; she might just as well stop trying. "About the cake?"

"Yes."

"Do you want to tell me now?"

"No." He leans forward as the jet slips beyond the window frame and out of view. "Where will it end up?"

Eleanor looks at the cake in its clear container and decides to offer him a piece later, once this mood, or whatever it is, lifts. "Did you talk to your girls today?" This snaps him out of his daydream.

"Oh yes, yes of course," he says, sky blue eyes settling on her. "And you? Did you talk to your boys?"

No time for that this morning, not while she was making the cake, she tells him, but she'll be in touch soon. "Any news from the girls?" Eleanor feels as if she knew Kelly and Emily and their families, even though they haven't met. How could they? They live in Japan. One day, perhaps.

"I hardly had time to talk to Kelly," Shane says. "Everyone was off doing something, deadlines to meet, hurrying and scurrying, just like those folks out there. Dashing around like chickens. All in a flap." He flicks his hand towards the window, out to the sidewalk and the endless flow of pedestrians.

"What's going on with Kelly?"

His face settles into deep thinking lines as he works through something. "Kelly's upgrading her financial license, and teaching more at the university. Since Michael's heart attack she's taken on more. The kids keep her hopping, as teenagers will do. They're planning a trip to see me. I told her that's the last thing they should be doing. I told her, go off on a vacation with Michael; never mind me. I'm well taken care of."

A while back, before Michael's health turned, Shane said he worried about Kelly's marriage. He thought all Michael's travel and Kelly's heavy workload, not to mention raising two kids, was too much. "It was nice of them to offer to come and see you, wasn't it?"

"Yes, I suppose so. But I'd rather they took care of themselves. Kelly's upset about Audrey, too. She's getting tattoos and apparently gives Kelly a lot of attitude. I told her it's normal. She doesn't like Audrey's new boyfriend either, but feels if she says too much it will have the opposite effect to what she wants." He raises his hands and laces his fingers together. "I suspect she's correct."

"What did you tell her?"

"Well, it's my understanding, judging by the staff here, that tattoos are all the rage. It doesn't make them bad people. Pick your battles, I told her. It's only skin; they're only pictures. As for the boyfriend, she knows how to handle it."

"Did you talk to Emily?"

"Oh yes. She's got her problems, too. A very mouthy, sarcastic son who she thinks is smoking marijuana. She suspects her daughter is anorexic or bulimic. Maybe both. Plus she's got a big job with her research, and her husband is flying all over the world with his work. Life is complicated these days isn't it?" He faces Eleanor, his heavy-lidded eyes filled with longing for a simpler time. "Don't you find it complicated?"

"Very." She tells Shane about her last Skype calls to her boys a few weeks ago, even though she's already told him before. No matter. They do this often, rehash stories. It's soothing, makes them part of something. "Everyone was in a hurry, no one with time to talk. Michael was running off to swimming lessons with his kids. Ian was jumping on a plane, headed off on a business trip." A grandmother in two dimensions, half-realized. Her grandchildren could see her, hear her, but she couldn't hold them, couldn't press her nose into their silken heads and smell them. What, they might wonder, would she have to do with them, this face that popped up from time to time, detached from its body, looming at them from its iPad tent on the kitchen table, like a ghost? Grandma by title only.

"Do you know, Emily talked about visiting me, too? She and Kelly are cooking up something together. They've got a big plan to all come at once with their families. I told her the same as her sister. Never mind jetting half-way 'round the world to see an old codger like me. I'm fine, well taken care of. I've no complaints. Emily said they might just surprise me."

Out the window, a woman walks by with a little white dog tugging on its leash, but Shane isn't watching her. He looks up into the sky, following the flight of another jet.

"Is it time for some cake?"

"Not today."

The quiver in his voice warns her against pressing him further. They visit a while longer, talk mostly about the beautiful fall weather, but Shane is not quite himself, more tired than usual. Eleanor says her goodbyes and gives the cake to a grateful staff member to take to the lunch room, requesting a piece be sent to Barb's mother. She wouldn't give up on trying to raise Shane's spirits.

***

At the pub, Barb leans over the table and asks why Shane refused to eat the cake, and why did Eleanor think he wouldn't tell her the whole story?

"Beats me," Eleanor says. "I thought I was doing something to free him of his pain, but I might have added to it. He seemed quite emotional when he saw the cake, I guess because of what happened."

Years ago, Shane's daughter Kelly, eight at the time, begged her mother to make her a daffodil cake for her ninth birthday party, since she'd had one at a friend's party. His wife set about to make it, an elaborate affair with angel food cake, lemon pudding and special fluffy white frosting. For days it was all Kelly would talk about, and on her birthday, when Shane's wife produced this magnificent cake, Kelly was over-the-moon.

All the children were meeting in the park, which had a petting zoo they'd visit after the picnic, games, and the present opening. All Shane had to do was deliver the cake, along with some of the gifts. On the way to the park, at the first corner, he heard a terrible crash and he suddenly realized he'd left the cake on the roof of the car. He pulled over, got out to see if anything could be saved, but the cake lay in the middle of the road, a pile of white and yellow mush, the plate shattered into a thousand pieces. He could hardly speak when he arrived at the park, and never in all his years of living, would he ever forget the look on Kelly's face when he told her what happened.

"That's not a big deal," Barb says. "Accidents like that happen all the time. We get over it."

"There's more," Eleanor reminds her. "But he won't tell me." She knows Shane feels things deeply, perhaps more than is healthy. Even the Cedar Grove staff comment on his sensitive nature and how he is a true gentleman.

"I'm not giving up. I'm baking another cake for our Wednesday visit."

***

Eleanor's second daffodil cake turned out better than her first one.

"You don't give up easily, do you?" Barb says when they meet, Eleanor holding the cake aloft.

"I still think it might help him get over his sadness about that birthday party so long ago."

"It's a cake, Eleanor. It's not magic."

***

Shane seems agitated as she takes her seat beside him, watches his hands twist restlessly in his lap. "Look at this." He points out the window, the sky a bigger canvas than before as high winds and rain of the last two days stripped the leaves off the trees, laying bare his view. "It's a sign," he says. "Universal restlessness. Souls crisscrossing our world, going who-knows-where?"

Eight jet trails stripe the sky in various stages of dissipation, the earliest ones shredded into faint strains of cotton batting, the newer ones solid and thick, laid down like fresh lines of paint. She sees cloudiness in his eyes she's never seen before, hears anxiousness in his speech. It's not like him to talk in abstract terms, almost metaphysical.

"There are a lot of planes today." She hopes she can bring him back into the room with her.

He bends forward, closer to the window. "Continuum," he says, as if he might be staring into eternity, and sits like that for a long time, until the spell breaks, and his glance alights on the cake. He leans back, his head resting against the chair, and closes his eyes.

"When I pulled up at the park and Kelly learned about the cake and how it had been destroyed, she behaved like a brat. She was rude to the other children. She told one to shut up and made another one cry by kicking her. She refused to play any of the games we planned for them. When it was time to open the presents, she ripped at the paper and tossed aside the gifts as if she hated them. We made her thank her guests. She gave them the most begrudging thanks you've ever heard. Do you know what I did?"

He turns to her, his half-open eyes blazing with fierceness. "What?" Her own boys often behaved badly at their birthday parties.

"I sent all the children home early, packed up the car, and took the family home. Kelly sat in the back, her arms crossed over her chest in defiance, kicking at the back of my seat, purposely trying to get my goat. I told her if she didn't stop right that instant she'd be going to her room as soon as we got home."

Eleanor can't imagine such harshness coming from him.

"When we got home, she called me a name. Something like, *you stupid idiot,* and I grabbed hold of her, pulled her to a chair, put her over my knee and spanked her.

My wife and Emily were horrified. They clung together and cried. I told them to stop, Kelly was a brat and she was getting exactly as she deserved. I hauled her to her room and locked the door, and for the next few hours she bashed and kicked it. I even refused to let my wife give her food for the rest of the day."

Eleanor can hardly believe what he's telling her. This sweet, considerate man, so devoted to his children.

Across the hall, Barb's mother's voice rises in her usual reign of protest, engulfing the hall, murdering silence with her list of grievances.

"I will have a piece of that cake now," Shane says.

Eleanor takes a knife from her bag and cuts off a generous slab. Perhaps telling the story rids him of a heavy burden of guilt. His hand trembles as he accepts the slice she holds out for him.

"Well, it is a masterpiece," he says. He rises from his chair, crosses the room, and heads out the door without so much as a word about where he might be going. Eleanor follows him into Barb's mother's room. He stands before her, a tiny wizened shape swallowed by a massive chair, her squawking voice reverberating around the room like the clatter of crows, as she attacks Barb.

"Madam," he interrupts, and her head rears back to take him in. "I am your neighbour from across the hall. I was wondering if you would do me the honor of sharing some of this fine dessert with me."

Barb's mother's face, pinched by rage, opens in astonishment at the spectacle of this plaid-shirted man, pants hoisted high by suspender straps, wearing bedroom slippers, standing before her with an offering of cake. No one, apart from Barb, ever visits her. Is it any wonder? Her voice sounds strange as she searches for a tone seldom used, and her eyes fall ravenously on the cake. "I suppose," she says.

Shane steps towards her, but does not bend to deliver the cake into her outstretched hand. "On two conditions," he says. "You need to lower your voice. I believe it's called finding your inside voice.

And the other one is you must stop being so nasty."

Barb's mother is stunned, as if someone has smacked across her cheek, or dumped cold water on her. Her head shakes in agitation and her face colours with rage. Her voice begins its climb to her usual pitch then tumbles down to a new register. "Okay." She sounds almost sweet, and garnishes her single word with the hint of a smile.

"I will come to see you tomorrow to hear how you enjoyed it." He places the plate on the armrest of her chair, turns and leaves the room, Eleanor in tow.

"I believe I would like a nap now," he says, sitting on the edge of his bed, then stretches out fully, one hand atop the other on his stomach, and closes his eyes.

***

Eleanor leaves the rest of the cake with the desk clerk. "For the staff," she says. "I'll pick up the container later. Please leave some for Shane and Barb's mom. But you are welcome to the rest."

At the pub, Barb says, "He was like an angel giving my mom a slice of sweet." She hasn't seen her mom so happy for a very long time and they order another carafe of wine to celebrate. Even Barb seems different after today's visit, not all bruised and beat up by her mother's abrasiveness.

***

Friday night, the phone rings. It's Nora Wilson, Chief Administrator from Cedar Grove, regretfully informing her Shane has passed. "Peacefully," she says. "Probably of a stroke. Some of the staff mentioned he might have been experiencing some episodes this week."

Eleanor can't think of what to say. Her thoughts fly to his family, the trip they were planning. "His children, his daughters, Kelly and Emily; they'll be devastated."

Perhaps Nora Wilson hasn't heard her; she is silent on the other end of the line, then she says, "You've a cake holder to pick up,

Eleanor. Could you come in tomorrow, let's say around two? I've got it in my office."

From her balcony, Eleanor stares at the Cedar Grove roof a few blocks away, sheds tears as she thinks of Shane. What will she do with her Wednesdays and Sundays, a selfish thought, she knows.

She calls Barb and arranges to meet her at the pub around four, after her appointment with Nora Wilson. Barb will know by Eleanor's faltering voice that she needs her.

***

Nora offers her a seat opposite her broad desk and places the cake container in front of her. "I imagine this comes as a shock to you, and I am sorry for your loss," she says. "I heard from the staff how close you and Shane were. He was a lovely, gentle man. He was very lucky to have you as a loyal visitor. Over a year, wasn't it?"

"Almost two." Eleanor dabs at her eyes. "It's so sad because his daughters were planning on coming. He told them no, but I have a hunch they were going to show up anyway, to surprise him."

"There's something I'd like to talk to you about," Nora says, as she pulls a folder out of her desk drawer. "We found some newspaper articles he had tucked away at the back of his cupboard." She shoves the folder across the desk towards Eleanor. "Read the top clipping."

Eleanor takes a yellowed newspaper page out of the folder. Dated back thirty-five years, the headline reads: *Japanese Jet Liner with 254 passengers disappears over the Pacific.* "Yes," Eleanor says, "I remember this. They never found it, did they?"

"Look farther down the page, at the article about the Vancouver sisters, two girls who were on that flight. See their names? Kelly and Emily."

"That is a huge coincidence," Eleanor says, and thought about it. "Did he name his daughters after them?" Even as she said this she knew it couldn't be, since the dates didn't add up. "So what are you saying?"

"Shane imagined the daughters. You know how sensitive he was.

It's as if he couldn't bear the pain of the sisters' death in the crash so he made up a life for them. It's the only explanation we've been able to come up with." Nora removes her glasses and settles back in her chair. "Our files show that he only had a wife and, of course, she was deceased. That's not all, I'm afraid. I know this is a lot to take in, but I need you to see something else." She slides a newspaper clipping across the desk.

Eleanor picks up the brittle paper and reads aloud, "Child killed on way to birthday party." She scans the article. A child, excited about going to a birthday party, ran out into the street into the path of an oncoming car and was killed instantly. No charges were laid against the distraught driver, Shane O'Connell.

No Kelly, no Emily, no cake. Had she, by bringing the cake, not once, but twice, forced him to a place he never wanted to go? A place he'd filled in long ago with a fantasy? And yet he held on to a bit of punishment, the bit about the spanking, his cruelty, unable to let go of the pain, a terrible reminder of killing a child.

***

By the time Eleanor leaves Cedar Grove on her way to the pub, the sky, clotted with pewter-coloured storm clouds, bears down, and the wind hurries leaves through the air. The occasional rain drop strikes her face; she pulls her scarf more snuggly around her neck.

She has to tell Barb. The story about Shane and his girls, a complete fabrication, the true story about the little girl he killed. An accident. Like her, Barb will have a hard time believing it, but she will eventually, as she comes to an understanding about how the mind invents, how it protects.

As she waits at the light, she thinks of going straight home, closing the curtains on the world, curling up on the couch, and standing Barb up. Then what? Hide for the rest of her life? No, she has to meet her, has to tell her everything. This moment cannot pass or her deception will be concealed even from herself, become as real to her as Shane's was to him, forever locking her away in her own solitude. And after telling her, what then? Would Barb still be her friend? How could anyone like someone so filled with such ridiculous pride?

Down the street, the sign for the Black Sheep Pub sways impatiently in the wind. Barb will be waiting. A glass of wine first, the news about Shane, give her time to process all of that, then the story about the poinsettia, her daughter-in-law, Sylvia, and Gabe, her little grandson.

Sylvia late as usual, the other two grandkids already there, dropped off by Eleanor's oldest son. Sylvia always came with a list of instructions about Gabe, her first child. *Don't feed him this, give him that, we don't use those words on him, your old toys are dangerous, his nap times are at* ..., as if she'd never raised two boys of her own. But even before Gabe, Eleanor found Sylvia off-putting, altogether too sure of herself. Condescending.

Sylvia started to cross the room to move the poinsettia away from the reach of the children—she'd read they could be poisonous. She'd put it on the counter, out of the way. Eleanor insisted no, Sylvia was running late, she should be off. She wore dress boots; she was going to tromp across the living room carpet to get the plant. Eleanor assured her she would take care of the plant straight away, and at the same time she thought, who was Sylvia to come into her home and tell her where to put things? And dirty the carpet with her boots.

Later, she ran into the bedroom for something, gone for mere seconds, and when she came back, Gabe was chewing a leaf. The convulsions seemed like they would never stop.

An accident, Eleanor told a distraught Sylvia as they sat at the child's hospital bedside for two days. But that wasn't enough for Sylvia. She demanded an apology. An accident, Eleanor pleaded. They all stopped talking to her, her entire family. Ian said none of them would speak to her again until she owned up to her carelessness. Gabe could have died.

Eleanor spots Barb in their usual booth and makes her way across the room. After she tells her the whole story, before Barb tells her what she must do, she will tell her plans to go across town to Ian's house, then to Aurora, north of the city, to visit Michael. She will apologize to all of them and ask for their forgiveness.

Even before the incident, she hadn't welcomed her daughters-in-law into her life. She'd criticized them, questioned them. How could they know her boys better than her? But they did, and she refused to let go. So filled with jealousy, so full of pride. And then she lost them all, as if they'd disappeared en route, dropped from the sky.

About the author:

Catharine Leggett's short stories have appeared in the anthologies *Law & Disorder*, *Best New Writing 2014*, *The Reading Place*, as well as in the journals *Room*, *Event*, *The New Quarterly*, *Canadian Author*, *The Antigonish Review*. Other stories have appeared in the online journal *paperbytes* and on CBC Radio. She is a two-time finalist in the Columbus Creative Cooperative Great Novel Contest and the winner of the Okanagan Fiction Award. New stories are forthcoming in KY Story and Per Contra. She taught creative writing in the continuing studies program for Western University, London, Ontario, Canada.

APPRENTICE AND MOTH
©2016 by William D. County

The apprentice tries to escape into a child in the crowd, or into Maria, or one of the dogs or cats prowling the nearby alleys, but the iron cuffs on his wrists bind his spirit in space as surely as they bind his body to the wooden post. Only the sergeant is close enough, but that man's mind is too strong to be supplanted. The sergeant places an eyeless black hood over the apprentice's head. It blocks light, but sounds remain all too clear as the man struts away, marching to the rhythm of his own boots on the cobblestone courtyard.

"Ready!" shouts the sergeant, followed by the clink and rattle of rifles rising.

"Aim!" shouts the sergeant. Time slows. An expectant hush falls over the crowd. Into the pool of silence, the apprentice dives backward in time. Hours pass, then days, then weeks swimming against the current as the sun travels west to east. He prays for a lifeboat.

A moth alights on the post.

***

The moth landed on the wooden post, a rest stop on its way to candlelit windows in the village. The moth shuddered as its awareness swelled with something larger than itself. Wings aflutter, it tried to escape, but the vast presence stilled its wings and banished the fear. Silent words of power echoed in the moth's rudimentary

119

consciousness, which faded like a dream upon awakening.

Two weeks. Two weeks to reach the Master, warn him, change history, and save himself. Little else fit into the tiny brain, so the spirit of the apprentice curled into a waking dream. The moth took flight, driven to follow the newly remembered trail to the home of the Shaman.

***

His last meal is hardly appetizing: beans, rice, and some jerky. The apprentice chews slowly, not tasting, not seeing, not hearing, yet he is fully alert, probing for a weakness. The iron bars of the cell frustrate him. The police know he studied under the Shaman, and they take no chances. He longs for some peyote, which would expand his mind beyond this cage. He'd settle for tequila, to dim the memories that shame him.

He swallows the food and lifts a glass of water to his lips. He pauses. Concentrates. He drinks and feels the burn of alcohol coat his throat. He pushes the food away and reclines on the cot. *I need the Shaman.* He laughs bitterly, closes his eyes, and dreams of flying.

***

The moth landed on a flower, extended its proboscis, and drank deep the intoxicating nectar. Dawn approached. Its wings drooped with weariness from flying throughout the night. Its brain felt numb with oft-repeated spells of ward against bats and other dangers. Fed but exhausted, the apprentice cast a spell of concealment. The moth slept, and dreamt of being a man.

***

"The defendant will please rise." The senior judge of the tribunal looks stern, a man of stone without a heart.

The apprentice stands, deliberately looking humble and helpless with his arms and legs in iron chains.

"Members of the jury, have you reached a verdict?"

"We have, your honor." The pause is a hen with two eggs: hope and fear. Which will hatch?

The apprentice studies the jurors' faces. None meet his gaze. They fear him. Only one person, a woman in the public gallery, stares back. Maria, the addle-minded whore barely capable of stringing three words together in proper order. The only witness for the prosecution. He turns from her smile to hide his fear.

He had thought the jury would scorn the testimony of a prostitute, but her calm, simplistic testimony had held the jury spellbound. Even the dark visions he sent to her—visions of rape, pain, and death—failed to shake her composure. She had changed since last he'd been with her, and not for the better.

"We find the defendant guilty of murder." The gavel sounds. The egg cracks.

***

Life was a blur of wings, an unending flight toward the goal. The Shaman was close, the smell of his garden more than an oasis recalled in dreams. Soon the apprentice would find help, release, and peace.

A different scent clamored for attention. His antennae quivered. The female moth flitted by, hijacking his neural pathways with her pheromones. He pursued, unable to resist. He mounted her, their wings fluttering as the female received his gift, continuing the cycle of their tiny lives.

Spent, he sent her away with a forceful nudge. He fought the contentment, the sense of fulfillment. He forced the primitive brain to concentrate, and summoned enough energy to form a protective spell. He needed sleep. He needed to remind himself of who he was.

***

Maria smells of too much perfume but the apprentice doesn't care. All he wants is some quick relief to settle his nerves. He pulls a gold coin from his satchel and flips it to her. She catches it, lifts it to her mouth as if to bite, but stops. She stares at the coin. "Blood?"

His fingers are still tacky. He glares as if it's her fault. "Tequila?"

She's still eying the coin. "Uh, in the kitchen?"

"Get it."

She buries the coin in the top dresser drawer beneath her undergarments, and ambles out of the room.

He goes to the water basin and rinses off the blood. His hands have no cuts. The mirror shows haunted eyes. He punches the face. *Now* his hand bleeds. Maria returns, shouting, "What's wrong, what's wrong?" waving an open bottle of tequila and spilling much of it on the floor.

The apprentice snatches the bottle and pours what's left down his throat. He wipes his mouth with the back of his arm. "Let's fuck."

They do.

The frenzied but unsatisfying coupling fails to relieve his anxiety. Intuition tells him to abandon his gold and flee. Impossible. The glitter calls to him. He will stay in the area, take over for the Shaman, and help the police with the investigation. Land and women are cheap here. He will buy an estate and live like royalty.

A knock sounds on the door. He grabs her arm and hisses, "Tell them to go away. You're not feeling well."

"I'm fine."

He slaps her face. The idiot stands there, rubbing her cheek. He spins her around and gives a shove. "Go."

He grabs his pants and hides in a closet, keeping door ajar to see anyone who comes into the bedroom. He pulls a dagger from a sheath on his belt.

Maria dons a robe and stomps to the living room. After a short, muffled conversation, she returns alone, carrying a potted plant. The apprentice releases a breath and slips the knife away.

Maria pouts. "This isn't flowers."

It looks familiar. "Who sent it?"

"The Shaman? But he always sends flowers."

"Not anymore." He grimaces, afraid he's said too much. A whore is dangerous—privy to secrets they're unable to keep. But Maria had a mind of a child and memory like a broken fence, unable to hold in much of anything. She probably couldn't remember his dick, let alone his face.

Maria touches the plant and shudders. When she turns to him her eyes are wary. "I know."

The accusation in her tone makes him think she really does know. His hand edges toward the hilt of the dagger. She smiles and lets her robe slide to the floor. He relaxes. Naked, she walks to the dresser and pats the top drawer. "Do you know why I have the gold?"

He runs from her house.

***

Dawn found the moth in the garden. The Shaman approached, walking beside a past echo of the moth's dreams. The Master knelt, his face glowing brighter than any flame. The moth hovered, basking in the light. The dream came fully awake.

Master, you are in danger.

I know.

I will die unless you stop me.

I know. The Shaman's hands moved, writing, tying. *I'm old. Time to find someone younger.*

I'm giving you a chance to change history, thought the moth.

Why would I want to do that?

The moth struggled to find the words. *Because I'm sorry.*

The Shaman whispered. "Remorse is not redemption."

***

The Shaman says, "This body is getting too old."

"I'm ready to take over, Master," the apprentice replies.

"I think not. Your skills blossom but your heart withers." He walks among the plants of the extensive garden. The apprentice follows. The apprentice knows the medicinal and psychic uses of every herb, root, and leaf. One plant serves no purpose; of it the Shaman would only shake his head and say some weeds have a mind of its own.

"My heart is strong, master. I'm in perfect health."

"Live among the poor and the homeless for a year. Come back then and I will see if you are ready."

"You might not last another year. As you said, your body is old. It is time for you to step aside, to enjoy your declining years in comfort while I take up the burdens of being Shaman."

"Give up all that you covet."

"I've studied with you for ten years. *Ten years.* I've already sacrificed. I'm ready to use my powers. For the good of mankind."

The Shaman draws a heavy sigh. "I grow tired of staring at the lies behind your face. Leave me."

"I will not go penniless. You owe me."

The master's gaze hardens but he says nothing. He kneels beside the useless plant. A moth hovers above it. The shaman stares at it a long time, then shakes his head sadly. He writes the name *Maria* on a delivery card, and ties it gently to the plant. He whispers something. The old fool has a soft spot for the dumb whore.

The Shaman stands. "I offer you what you offer me. Salvation. Forsake all that you have and leave."

"You have a stash of gold coins. Give me half, in payment of my time and service."

"Ah," says the Shaman. "Do you know why I have that gold?"

"Because you're a greedy old goat like everyone else."

"I have no use for gold," says the old man, his voice low, weighed down by untold years. "Like everything in life, it is merely another test."

The apprentice looks around. It's as if fate provided this moment for him. They are alone. The grounds are devoid of birds, dogs, snakes, animals of any kind. Even the moth has vanished. He picks up a garden hoe. The impact with the Shaman's head is jarring but satisfying; the master lies still, blood oozing from the cracked skull. The apprentice runs to a nearby shed and returns with a length of iron chain to bind the Master's spirit. It's bloody, tiring work. He watches the man die, then takes all the gold. An unexpected erection strains his pants.

***

All for naught. The smell of death permeated the air. He had now but one chance—to find a new host, preferably some child of weak mind to possess. But the moth was old now, and its strength was failing. He would not survive the flight back to the village.

Perhaps it didn't need to.

Maria.

It was so obvious, so easy. The moth would hitch a ride on the plant, be delivered to her door, and take up permanent residency in her almost empty head. Realization flashed through his mind. Of course Maria had been composed at the trial: *he was already inside her.* And the weirdness in the bedroom, her reference to the gold, that was her way of hinting that the transfer was made. She—he— couldn't risk saying more for fear of changing the future. She'd been at the execution, too, her grim face belying the joke he'd played on himself!

With relief, the moth settled down to rest on the plant.

Bars sprang up on all sides, trapping him. He threw himself against the green cage, knocking powdery flakes from his wings. The bars did not yield.

The stinging began. A burning hell fire dissolved his legs.

He tried to send out his spirit, but found nothing to receive it.

This can't be happening. I'm dreaming. I'm dreaming.

Yes, said the Venus Flytrap in the voice of the Shaman. *So am I.*

About the author:

W. D. County (Dave) enjoys writing speculative fiction, often with a touch of irony. He has a keen appreciation for technology, drawing on experience as a nuclear reactor operator aboard the ballistic missile submarine *USS Sam Houston* (SSBN 609), more than a decade as a quality assurance manager at the Three Mile Island Nuclear Station, and nearly two decades as a custom software developer for the federal government and several major companies. His publication credits include the techno-thrillers *Sammi* and *Oasis at the Bottom of the Sea*, as well as short stories in the e-zine *Spinetingler* and anthologies *Speedloader*, *Pulp Ink 2*, and the *Aesthetica Creative Writing Annual 2014*. His nonfiction includes articles in *Lotus Advisor* and *Contact* magazines. Dave holds a Master of Fine Arts degree in writing from Lindenwood University and currently teaches composition at Brown Mackie College in Kansas City, Missouri.

SATURDAY NIGHTS IN WINTER
©2016 by Jennifer A. Powers

If you drained the Jackson River, you'd probably find beat-up cars, jewelry, unregistered guns, photos, letters, suitcases, underwear, shoes, and an infant's skeleton in a cloth sac. Lower- to middle-class housing and commercial buildings were erected on both sides of the river, and there, in a shadowy crevice, flashed the red and white beer signs of my mother's favorite restaurant/bar, where she met up with The Lover. As we drove across the Millstone Bridge in the blue station wagon, I stared at the fast-flowing, icy water below us. The Millstone Bridge was an old bridge, yet sturdy, with steady traffic speeding across it. But one step in the wrong direction on a dark night....

A dizzy sensation overcame me—I could open the car door and fling myself out. I could test my mother's love. I could see if she'd swerve into traffic by trying to grab me. I could see if she'd stop the car or continue to the bar. I placed my hand on the door handle and felt the winter outside. I could tell her I'd jump out if we didn't turn around and go home. I could threaten to tell Dad if she didn't listen. But I remained silent and felt my hand go numb.

They'd fought before she dropped him off at the train station. Her face had been tense, in agony. On the way to the bar, she seemed to barely grip the steering wheel, relaxed and at ease, unlike being at home where she was always trying to please Dad, cook for Dad, massage Dad's feet. Mom would say, "What about *my* feet?" and Dad would say, "Until you work, my feet are the only ones that matter," and Mom would say, "Working means paychecks and we're broke," and Dad would slap her across the cheek. But instead of crying, she'd smirk, lift her head, and stare at him like he wasn't even there, and I knew what she was thinking. She was thinking about our secret. She was thinking about The Lover and how Dad didn't know about him.

We lived in a trailer by the Jackson River. We didn't have neighbors where we lived so no one heard the yelling and the slapping. No one saw me hiding. I'd linger along the river's edge, the Jackson River that ran right out of town, and I wondered if it could take me with it. I could build a raft and be like Tom Sawyer and Huck Finn. In summer, I'd pick daisies and make mud pies and dip my feet in the water to kill time. In winter, I'd be Wonder Woman and turn a long branch into my lasso to fight off the bad guys. Then I'd jog up the little wooded pathway and go back inside when I thought it was over. Dad worked in sales and went away a lot. Mom met up with The Lover on Saturday nights for several months. "Traveling salesman," she'd tell The Lover. "Selling what, I don't know. Spending it all on bottles of Jack. I've had it."

The back roads to the bar were curvy and dark. It started to snow. I looked at my mother's pale blonde hair teased with Aqua Net and molded into tiny S-shaped curls. The soft light from the dashboard calmed her face. She had big blue starlet eyes and they grew three sizes on those Saturday nights. "Don't fall in love," she'd say. "It's messy."

My mother cupped my chin. We were almost at the bar. "What, honey? You seem to be in another world?"

"I want to go home. I don't want to go to that place," I said.

"We talked about this. These are our secret adventures. I'm trying to make things better for us," she said.

"I'm old enough to stay home alone."

"You're ten years old. Absolutely not." She blushed, relaxed. "How about we get ice cream after?"

"I hate ice cream."

"You *love* ice cream," she said.

"I hate ice cream *today*. I hate ice cream on Saturdays."

We pulled into the restaurant/bar parking lot, alone with my secrets, and alone with the one we shared. The bar reeked of stale beer and cheap cologne. The Lover placed a handful of coins in my palm and my mother told me to check out the arcade in the game room in the restaurant area. Some long-haired, pimply teenaged boys hogged Pac Man and Donkey Kong. I sat alone at a sticky table, cross-armed, ready to fight the group of boys if they asked why I was on their turf. I hated everyone.

***

We celebrated Thanksgiving at church. They roasted turkeys in the basement kitchen and stirred up some instant mashed potatoes and opened a couple cans of cranberry sauce. Other families who had "money troubles" joined us. Dad bought me Garbage Pail Kids cards for Christmas, and Mom got mad, saying, "Why'd you get a young lady that trash?"

"I wanted them," I'd said. I gave her a chilly glare. I'd tell Dad about our secret. She calmed down, lit a cigarette, and waved her hand.

"When did you start smoking?" Dad had asked. She just waved her hands and walked away.

The holidays passed and it seemed colder, unbearable, below-zero wind chills, starless skies, three-foot icicles, whipping winds, and crystallized snow (not wet and warm like it was in early winter when things still felt hopeful around the holidays). It was a frozen white wilderness. A few days after New Year's, we made another trip over the bridge to the bar to meet up with The Lover. He'd bought me a Christmas gift: a porcelain doll. It looked like me: long black hair, brown eyes, pale skin. It wore a wedding gown. The Lover had money. He drove a red sports car and it smelled like cigars. Mom kept her wedding bands in her purse when she met The Lover, but he left his on. It was gold. I thought gold meant things didn't break. He clasped a diamond necklace around my mother's neck and she looked like a child as he was doing it. I dropped the porcelain doll on the floor and the face cracked down the middle. I grinned, looked up, and my mother shook me.

"You did that on purpose!"

"I did not!" I said.

"You're lying."

"You're the liar," I said. "I'm never getting married." I kicked the porcelain doll wearing the wedding gown.

"Girls, girls," The Lover said. "It's the holiday season. Let's not get hot. I'll buy her one she likes. No biggie."

"I don't want another one," I said.

"See? She does things on purpose," my mother said. She appeared panicked. "I'm sorry," she said to The Lover. She rubbed his arm, kissed his cheek. She bent over and said, "Honey, let's have a seat. I'll get you some strawberry milk. Your favorite." She took my hand. "I'm sorry for getting so upset."

"Allow me," The Lover said, pulling out a fifty dollar bill.

***

The day felt sad. The early morning sun sliced through the bare trees. The pink clouds reminded me of my mother's peonies in summer. I found myself on The Lover's couch, locked out of the bedroom where my mother slept with The Lover. The wind pressed against the house. The Lover's wife had moved out. I got up, knocked on the bedroom door.

"Go lay back down, honey," my mother said.

"I'm cold," I said. "I want to go home."

The Lover grumbled. I banged harder. The night before I kept hearing the word "divorce" and "settlement."

"Honey—go lay back down for a little while," my mother said.

"I don't feel good. I wanna go home."

"Soon."

***

I climbed my favorite pine tree by the river rapids, observing the landscape from a high up tree branch. I could see our trailer. I could see them coming to look for me. We had to go to the train station to drop off my father. I wrapped my legs around the thick limb and stretched out my arms. I closed my eyes and pretended to be a bird. I listened to the way the river sounded like a waterfall, powerful and fast. The sun spotlighted me. "Allow *me*! Let's get ice cream! I'll get her another one." I loved making fun of them. I stuck out my tongue and spit.

"Get down from there. We have to bring your father to the station," my mother said from below.

"I'm not going!" I said.

"Get down."

"No."

"Your father'll miss his train. Do you want that?" she asked.

"Yes!"

"Get down."

"What's the matter with her?" my father asked, coming down the wooded pathway. He wore a cheap suit the color of our rusty sink. "I need to catch a train. Get the hell down." He paced. He put his hands on his hips. "If you don't come down now you'll be sorry when you do. And, by God, you know I mean it."

My mother had her head down. I climbed down. I rushed past them, hating them, buckling myself into the backseat of the station wagon. I heard them arguing from a distance. It was another Saturday. I knew where we were going after we dropped off my father. They got in the car and a silence swept over us. There was nothing left to say.

***

My mother liked to say "Tonight is the night" as she powdered her nose, sipped wine from the box, slipped on pantyhose. I decided to steal the phrase.

"Tonight is the night," I said to myself. I picked the night of escape to the Millstone Bridge to test her love, to see if she'd look for me. "Tonight is the night." It was just another Saturday night in winter.

At the restaurant/bar that night, The Lover tried too hard to make me laugh. He bought me Shirley Temples with extra cherries. He had wet lips and glinting eyes like a snake's, black too, pulling coins out of my ears and giving them to me, telling me to "show those older boys how to play the game right," practically shooing me away. But I just stood there, pocketing the money. I rubbed the sweaty coins between my fingers. I ate the cherries and they tasted like The Lover's dirty coins.

Tonight is the night.

My mother and The Lover, with his wild hair and wet lips and glinting eyes, held each other hurrying to the red sports car. I tagged along. The Lover's dirty money jingled inside my coat pocket. I slipped on a patch of ice but they didn't notice until my mother reached the car and I wasn't behind her. Then she saw me on the ground.

"What on earth are you doing?" she asked.

But I just remained on the ground, staring at her. She hurried over, lifted me up. "Are you all right?" My eyes welled up. My lips quivered. "Oh, honey, don't cry. You know I love you. This has nothing to do with you," she said. I hated that she was being nice.

At The Lover's house, my mother laughed like she was being tickled. I stood in the doorway, watching. "Mom and Dad still do it, you know," I said. It went quiet. The only thing I heard was the sound of fizzy beer being poured into glasses.

"Stop it!" my mother said. She turned to The Lover, "She doesn't know what she's talking about."

"That true?" The Lover asked. "You sleeping with him—*and me?*"

"No. No! We just sleep in the same bed." My mother slapped my face. "Go to bed!"

The Lover got out my blanket and my pillow (without the pillowcase). My mother remained in the kitchen. They talked low for a while and then I heard them kissing. They clinked glasses.

"To us."

"To us," my mother said. "A new beginning. Thank you for

understanding."

"Of course," The Lover said.

My mother came into the living room and kissed my forehead. I pretended to be asleep. They disappeared into The Lover's bedroom. I heard the door lock and I was left alone with the cold, blue moonlight pouring through the bay window.

Tonight is the night.

I got up, put on my shoes and coat, and left the house. I threw a rock through The Lover's bedroom window so they'd get up, so they'd notice I was gone, so they'd come looking for me. The Millstone Bridge wasn't far. I memorized the route, Saturday after Saturday, month after month. It was so cold, but I believed it would all be worth it. My mother would reach out for me as I pretended to jump off the bridge when I saw her coming. I'd watch her pale blonde hair blow up and down in the winter wind like an erratic halo. She'd run toward me, yelling my name. I could save us. We'd never have to see The Lover again.

But I slipped on an icy patch halfway across the bridge, and as I reached out for the railing or anything to grab onto, my body was already hitting the Jackson River. I felt like shattered glass. The water felt alive, more alive than me, more alive than the angriest human being. But it was emotionless, perhaps unearthly, a presence so cold, it boiled, burning my skin and making me swallow its briny, metallic taste. I couldn't yell. I couldn't flail. I sunk with the thought of my beautiful mother warm and safe and stupid in The Lover's bed, while The Lover searched outside for a possible intruder. She didn't come.

But I was right. After that Saturday night in winter, after the Jackson River swallowed my body and nothing was found except my coat that finally washed ashore with The Lover's coins still inside the pocket, my parents divorced, and my mother and The Lover disintegrated.

At least I saved her.

About the author:

Jennifer A. Powers resides in New England. She earned a BA in

English and an MFA in Creative Writing. She has short stories published or forthcoming in *The MacGuffin*, *Folio*, *Diverse Voices Quarterly*, *Grasslimb*, *Hawai'i Pacific Review*, among others. She is at work on a book and she loves hiking, art, and coffee. Please visit jennpowers.com.

WAVES
©2016 by Michelle Wotowiec

It was a Wednesday night and I was training a new girl, Happy, how to serve. She was to shadow me for the night, and if I gave her the approval, she would be put on her own for tomorrow's shift. This was Happy's third day of training, but first day on the floor dealing with customers. It was all computer work and menu work up to this point. I heard from some of the girls that she was trying to leave an abusive husband and was in desperate need of the money.

"Is there anything you need to ask me, or is there anything about this place that you're not comfortable with yet?" I asked Happy while we filled twenty ramekins with ketchup. I wondered if she chose to wear long sleeves in order to cover the bruises. I knew a few girls who did that.

"Not really," she said. Her long black hair was pulled back, displaying gorgeous blue- and red-gemmed Middle Eastern earrings.

"Do you like it so far?" I asked.

She hesitated, "It isn't so bad. To be honest, though, I just *really* need the money."

"If you give it a chance, it's worth it. Trust me," I smiled, trying to ignore the red flag she just gave me. I had consciously decided to stop judging people.

"I know I am going to have to work more than one job to get where I need to be. It's too bad we can't just get rich waiting tables, you know?"

"Yeah, for sure," I responded. I didn't tell her just how much money I was actually making at the restaurant; it would have blown her mind.

"I've been stuck in a rut for a while and I'm just ready to get out of it. My parents offered to let me move back in with them, but that's back in the Middle East."

"Oh wow," I said. Eight or nine cliché pictures of the Middle East flashed in my mind. "Don't you have anyone here who can help you out for the time being?" I didn't want to pry too much, so I tried to stay vague.

"No, just Richie." The two had supposedly met at an AA meeting. That's what she told the other girls, anyway. What she was doing in the States all by herself being an alcoholic was something I might have asked her, but like I said, I was working on not judging anyone. If her story had holes in it, so be it.

We were silent as we finished filling the ketchups.

"How long have you been here?" she asked, putting the focus of the conversation on me.

"Since we opened last year," I said, surprised that almost a year had already passed.

"What about before that?"

"I've been serving since I was sixteen. I started at a Denny's and then went to a Damon's Grill. I was there for years before I got lucky and got this job."

I didn't tell her about the master's degree I was sitting on because I couldn't find a job. Or maybe I just couldn't get myself to look hard enough. I let her, and everyone else in the restaurant, think the restaurant was all I had.

"How do you do it? I serve for a year and have to take a break before coming back. It's a hard job."

Another red flag: what was the point of hiring a girl who was only going to stay for a short time? I said, "It's funny, whenever someone asks me this I always remember the girl who trained me at Denny's. She said, 'You are a server because you like people. If you don't like people, then don't serve.'" I didn't tell her that I had run into that woman a few weeks back working at a gas station. Her hair wasn't brushed, she had dark circles under her eyes, and she appeared to be seven or eight months pregnant with still no ring on her finger.

Happy laughed, "If that's the case, I don't think we'd have a lot of servers."

"Fair enough. I will alter her statement a little bit and say that you have to *want* to like people." I *did* like people. In general, I liked people. I wasn't sure if this was something I chose to do, or something I did innately, but I knew it was what got me through the night.

"Two at six hundred," Marybeth mouthed to me from across the bar as she made her way back to the hostess stand.

It was only ten minutes after five. Last Wednesday, my first table didn't come in until almost six. I'd made it a habit that any table coming in after three would be greeted with glasses of ice water. It saved me the trip back to the soda station and it usually impressed them that I was one step ahead of the game.

"Hi there, how are you?" I asked the elderly woman sitting at the table as I placed the two glasses of water down, spilling just a few drops. I quickly wiped them up with a napkin that I kept in my apron.

She turned from the window and looked up at me. Her skin drooped down her face, partially hiding her grey eyes. Her cheeks were pink with blush and her eyelashes were lined in blue mascara that matched the small vase of flowers displayed on the table. "I'm well, thank you. And how are you?" Her voice was soft but scratchy.

"I'm great, thanks," I smiled. "My name is Shelly and this is Happy, we'll be taking care of you. Have you been here before?"

"Happy?"

"Yes, my name is Happy," Happy smiled at the woman. From her left, I admired her defined cheekbones and small nose. I would trade her noses in a second.

"What a unique name! It just might be the most beautiful name I've ever heard. I think you have great things in store for you, dear."

"Have you been here before?" I asked again.

"Oh no, no, no," she looked down to her shaking hands and hid them underneath the table.

"Okay, great. I'm glad you came in. Want me to tell you a bit about the menu?" A lot of people were intimidated by the choices—worded a bit difficultly and some of the options such as chicken livers and chicken and waffles not being too user friendly. Not to mention going over the menu with the woman would help out Happy.

"No, not yet, Shelly. My friend will be here soon and maybe you can help the two of us at once. In the meantime, I will take the ribeye dinner."

"How would you like that prepared?" My mentor at Denny's had taught me to say 'prepared' rather than 'done.' Asking how someone would like that 'done' sounded hick-ish and improper, she'd said.

"Medium rare, please."

"Okay, we'll get this started right away for you and come back shortly," I said.

"Okay."

"Sounds like a plan to me," I began to walk away.

"Would you like anything to drink in the meantime?" Happy had stayed behind.

"Just a coffee, please," she smiled and waited for the two of us to turn away before looking back out the window.

***

"That's a cute little lady you have up there at six hundred," Kathy said to Happy and me at the soda station as I started a fresh pot of coffee. "I hope I am still going out on dates when I'm that old."

"Yeah, a cute little lady with a big appetite," I laughed, looking over my shoulder as I placed the coffee cup directly below the dripping coffee. "She ordered the ribeye."

"Well, I have a not-so-cute old lady at four-oh-six," Meg chimed in. "I asked her if there was anything I could help her with and she said 'You can help me figure out why I am here.'"

"Are you kidding?" Kathy asked.

I didn't join the bitchfest. I had been thinking about aging a lot lately. An eighty-something-year-old woman, like the one at 406, didn't have as much time to work with as we did. Well, if the world plays by the rules and doesn't throw any curveballs, that is. She could go at any minute. I imagined her son had dragged her into this gastropub thinking she would find something she liked. She, though, glanced over the menu and didn't see whatever it was she was in the mood for and realized she was wasting her time—the little time she had left.

The past two weeks I had been finding myself letting the elderly cut me in the checkout lines of Giant Eagle. Same principle. I had a lot more time to kill buying groceries than they did.

"Three at six-oh-seven, Shell," Marybeth said from behind me.

"Thanks," I smiled back. I poured three waters and put them on a tray with the old woman's coffee.

"It's hot, so be very careful," I said, placing it safely onto her table before turning around and heading over to 607.

"Hi there, how are you tonight?" I smiled as I placed the waters down. Happy stood close behind.

"We're good," a man with dark brown hair said. He appeared to be with his wife and child.

"I brought three waters, would you like me to put his in a plastic cup?"

"Oh no, Jeremy will be fine. Won't you, Jeremy?"

Her son, probably about six or seven years old smiled as he saw that he had a glass in front of him. "Yes, I'll be careful."

I left 607 to look at the menus and come up with any questions they might have for me. Meanwhile we made our way back to my lady at 600.

"Are you sure we can't get anything else for you while you wait for your friend?" I tried not to stare at the blue flowers she had taken from the vase and wrapped in her gray hair.

"Oh, no thanks. I'm just enjoying my coffee."

"Okay, well, let me know if I can help at all."

I was hoping her friend would come in before the dinner rush did.

Women of their age always took up the most time.

***

Twenty minutes later I was placing chicken and waffles, lump crab mac and cheese, and a grilled cheese sandwich onto 607 when Jeremy said, "Look, Mom. That old lady is waving at the cars."

"Shush, Jeremy. That's rude."

"How does everything look for you?" I knew it looked perfect as I had inspected it before bringing it out to the table, another thing my mentor had taught me. *Always know that there won't be problems, it will save you a lot of time*, I can almost hear her say. To my right I saw Marybeth seat a couple at 603.

"Looks great," the husband and wife said in unison.

"Look, Mom, she is *still* doing it!" Jeremy was laughing hysterically.

"*Jeremy Michael,* what did I just tell you?"

I placed my tray below my elbow and made my way to 603. The woman was gorgeous with her long blonde hair and navy dress. The man was equally attractive.

"Hi there, how are you tonight?" I smiled.

"We're great," the woman said warmly, letting go of her date's hands and placing hers at her side.

"Great. Have you been here before?" This question, I admit, got old fast, but we were a relatively new restaurant.

"Yes, quite a few times," her date said as he opened the drink menu.

"Awesome. It's great to have you back. Do you know what you would like to drink, or would you like a minute to decide?"

"I'll take a Kentucky Bourbon Ale," the woman said.

"Same," her date closed the menu and placed it aside.

"All right, I'll get these for you and I'll be back. Let me know if you have any questions."

Before leaving my station, I stopped at table 600 where my lady continued to wave at the cars driving past. Happy was saying something to her that I couldn't quite make out.

"Everything okay?" I asked, knowing I didn't have more than a minute to kill. I was beginning to think she was lost, and she hadn't touched her ribeye.

"Oh, yeah. Just waiting."

"Do you like the ribeye?" I asked, hoping Happy had already addressed the issue.

"Oh, yes dear, it's absolutely wonderful," she smiled.

I went to the first TwoTouch station, but Kathy appeared to be putting through her sixteen top's order. I looked to the right and saw the second TwoTouch was free. I put in the Kentuckys and filled four more glasses of water while I watched Marybeth coming from my station, mouthing me that she had to double seat 601 and 602. I didn't care. I loved being double sat. More people meant more money, something that my Denny's mentor didn't have to teach me.

"Food runner!" Chef yelled from the kitchen, "I need a runner!"

I looked at my drinks at the bar and the drinks I had just filled. I wasn't sure where Happy was. If I didn't run the food, I wouldn't hear the end of it. I had the reputation for relying too heavily on the food runner. I placed the glasses aside and went into the kitchen. The heat engulfed me instantly as I looked at Jeff and Gerry on the line covered in sweat. Chef's face was beet red. There had to be twenty tickets on the line.

"Take it! Take it!" he yelled as I grabbed a chicken salad and a strip steak.

As I took the food to 102, I saw that we were on a wait. This meant that my section was full. I was going to need eleven waters and to grab those beers. Oh, and I needed to bring napkins to Jeremy at 607. I had meant to do that.

"Fuck!" Kathy yelled as she went into the server cooler, "where is the ranch?!"

"Check the bottom shelf," I said as I made my way past her with a full tray. The beers were going to have to wait. There was no way I'd be able to make them fit on this tray. The bar crowd had grown considerably and I had to weave through people to get to my section.

Just then, the owner was next to me:

"What can I do to help?"

"Run the Kentuckys, please," I smiled as I continued to balance the tray. The 600s was the furthest section from the kitchen and soda station. Needless to say, I'd become a professional at multi-tasking.

Once in my section, I saw that my lady at 600 was still alone, only now she was standing, facing the window. Jeremy was waving at me with his empty glass of Pepsi. Happy had already gotten two of the tables waters. I decided to start at 601 and work my way over. The Pepsi could wait a minute. I didn't have time to ask who was sat first, but ultimately it didn't matter. I would end up treating it like one big party table. This would be very efficient for both the customers and myself, but it would piss off the kitchen. They hated tickets being stacked one after another. I wouldn't have been surprised if Chef stopped me personally in the middle of it all and ripped me a new one.

After every customer had a glass of water in front of them I saw that Happy had gotten the Pepsi and the napkin for Jeremy. I went back to 601 and started taking the orders, "Thanks again for waiting. As you can see, we filled up pretty quick."

"Oh, no problem," a woman around my age said to me. She was here with her mother, she said, and they had plenty of catching up to do. I could take my time.

Finally, I made it to table 606. "Thanks for waiting, how are you tonight?"

"I don't understand any of this," the man said. He had a large mole on his right cheek and a full head of gray hair.

"We need suggestions," his wife said without making eye contact with me.

"Okay, no problem. Is there any kind of food you don't like?"

"Just make suggestions," the woman repeated dryly.

I again remembered what my mentor had said to me, *You are a server because you like people*, so I smiled. "Okay, then, I suggest the salmon. It is seven ounces and comes from Scotland."

"Does it come with soup?" her husband asked. I noted a large chunk of dry skin above his right ear.

"No, we don't actually have any soup tonight—"

142

"No soup?" This is the first time the woman had looked at my face. Her eyes looked dry and her lipstick was too dark.

"No, we only do soup at lunch time."

"Well what does it come with?"

"Garlic whipped potatoes," I placed my finger on the menu in front of him where it clearly described the side included.

"Oh, well, you like mashed potatoes, Tom," she sounded frustrated as she shoved her menu toward me. I felt bad, but I knew I was too busy for the feeling to last long.

"We'll both take that," the old man said and quickly dismissed me.

Before making my way to the TwoTouch, where there was sure to be a line, I stopped at 600. "Do you need me to call your friend for you?"

She shook her head. She was standing now, staring at the other tables in my section with her arms crossed.

"Why don't you sit back down?" I asked as nicely as I could. I was afraid the owner would see her and ask her to leave.

"I—"

"Is there anything I can get for you?"

"Yes. I'll take the salmon," she said, smiling, as she found her seat and turned back toward the window.

"No problem, I'll get that right in," I said, assuming the meal was for her friend.

Twenty minutes later I was back in the kitchen: "Michelle, you're up like fifty times. Don't go far." Chef was mad, but held his temper the best he could.

"Don't make that chicken and waffles!" Kathy yelled into the kitchen from the server alley. "Don't make the chicken and waffles!"

"Why doesn't it say *don't make* underneath it!" Chef blurted.

"I already started it!" Gerry yelled.

"We can sell it, there are fifty chicken and waffle orders!" Jeff chimed in. The heat was almost unbearable.

"Start running!" Chef yelled. "Get the fuck out of here!"

It took me a second to realize he was talking to me. I grabbed the ticket and examined the order for 601.

"This needs sweet potato fries," I said as I grabbed two sides of ketchup, a ranch, and a side of Dijon mustard.

"Heard!" Chef yelled back, taking the regular fries and tossing them in the trash.

Once the food was ready, I stepped out of the kitchen and felt the immediate relief of the air conditioning.

After all of the tables had their food, I did one more run through to make sure everyone was content.

I saw Happy standing frozen at 601 in tears. "What's the problem?" I asked.

"Excuse me, but this was supposed to be *medium rare*," the woman said to me regarding her strip steak, a twenty-dollar dish.

"I'm so sorry," I said as I took a few steps to the shelves where I had side plates stashed. "If you will just put the steak on this plate, we will get it fixed right away. You can work on your fries and veggies until I bring it back."

"No. No you won't. I don't want it anymore."

I looked at the wrinkles on her forehead and the coffee stain on her blouse. I wondered how she had become who she became. Was it something genetic—something inevitable? Or did she live a miserable life that eventually caught up with her; a miserable life that eventually won her over, leaving her as this mean woman bitching at her server over a piece of food?

"Happy, why don't you go check and see if anyone needs another drink?" I wanted to get her out of it. It was my table and my bullet to take.

"Excuse me!" the man at 603 snapped his fingers to get my attention. "Am I getting that bottle of wine or what?"

"Don't go over there, Happy, I'll handle it. Actually, why don't you go run food?"

"Okay," she managed to spit out before she walked away, wiping away tears.

"One second," I said to the man at 603 and forced a smile. "Are you sure I can't get this recooked for you?"

"I've lost my appetite," she was a heavyset woman. Her lips were painted bright red and her arms were crossed. "And while you're at it, make that poor old woman stick her tongue back in her mouth."

I looked over at 600 to see the woman sticking her tongue out at Jeremy. Both the ribeye and the salmon sat untouched on the table.

"Look, Mom!" I heard Jeremy yell from 607.

"My bottle?" The man was growing more irritated by the second. "Can't you see I'm on a date here?" His date was about half his age. She was probably younger than I was. I had assumed he was her father.

I took note of all of the refills, got more drink orders, and made my way to the bar. The bottle wasn't up.

I found the owner and explained the steak situation and made my way back to the drink station.

"We don't have the Red Blend," Mandy yelled to me from the taps across the bar.

"Shit," I looked to my right and saw a man in his twenties smile at me. He was wearing a backward blue baseball cap and a black button-down shirt.

"You're cute," he said before I had walked back over to 603.

"I'm so sorry, sir, we don't have the Red Blend." I forced myself to make eye contact with the man. I wondered if it was too many moments just like this one that had left my once mentor as a clerk at a gas station, making a fifth of what we made at the restaurant. Maybe it was moments like this one that redefined the value of money.

"What do you mean you don't have it?"

"Just order us something else, Greg." I could tell his date was getting embarrassed.

"We sold out of it," I managed to respond. Back during my Denny's days, I probably would have been crying while he talked down to me. I was older now, and while I wasn't crying, I still felt like I was losing something.

"Maybe you should tell your managers to keep a better inventory," he clasped his fingers together and placed his hands on the table. "Why don't you tell me what I am supposed to do now?"

I was sure he was about to lose his temper. "Is there something else I can get for you?" He no longer had my full attention. It was my innate way of dealing with people like him: my survival instinct had finally kicked in. I scanned the other tables to see how things were going.

"Yeah, another type of red blend."

"We only carry the one." To my left I saw that the lady at 600 had taken her shoes off and placed them on the empty chair across from her.

"Well, then, we're just out of luck, aren't we?"

"One second," I smiled and walked back to the bar.

The man in the blue baseball cap was waiting for me. "Haven't seen you here before," he said louder than necessary.

"I've been here," I smiled back.

"So do you like it?" he asked, not quite so loud. His hand shook as he reached for his beer on the bar.

"I need something for this red blend guy, Mandy, he is being a royal jerk."

"What about a cab?" Mandy was pouring a Left Hand Milk Stout.

"Yeah, can I get a taster of the Villa Mt. Eden?"

"You didn't have the wine some guy wanted?" The blue-capped man chimed back in.

"No, go figure," I smiled.

"Want me to take care of him for you?" He smiled and took a large swig of beer.

"I think I can handle it," I said as I took the sample from Mandy and made my way back to table 603.

"That'll have to do, I guess," the man said after he took the sip of wine, "but I'll be needing to talk to your manager before I leave."

***

The rush was finally starting to die down when I remembered to go back to table 600. Happy was sitting across from the woman.

"...just don't know what to say," Happy finished saying.

"Be brave, young lady," the woman reached over the table and took Happy's hand in hers.

"Is there anything else I can get you while you wait?" I asked, assuming she had to be starving by that point. The food was still untouched.

"Yeah, why don't you surprise me with something sweet?"

"Well, is there any desserts you don't like?"

"Cats."

"What?"

"I don't like cats for dessert. Anything else will be fine."

I laughed and assured her we didn't serve cats—this wasn't China after all. She didn't smile.

Back in the server alley, Kathy was bitching about some campers, "One-oh-one sat there for *three* hours. I'm not fucking with you, *three hours.*"

"Well, did they tip you okay?" I responded as I scanned the TwoTouch screen deciding what to order for table 600.

"They each spent fifteen dollars and tipped me two-fifty."

"I'm sorry, that sucks."

"No, it really does suck. Do you know how much money I could have made if that table had flipped the three or four times that it should've?" Kathy ranted. We had all done this rant so it was only polite to hear it through.

"I know." A crème brulee—that would be perfect for her.

"I think I saw your trainee with her hair down," I heard Meg say from what sounded to be the kitchen.

I had noticed she'd taken her ponytail out. I didn't want to say anything in front of the lady at 600. Happy had worked in the industry before, I was sure she was aware of the health code.

"I *never* do that when I go out. *Never.*" Kathy was still fuming about her campers. I figured I'd give her another five minutes and she'd get past it, at least past the verbal acknowledgement of it anyway.

"Where is your trainee, anyway?" Meg asked from the kitchen where she was washing her hands. I had overheard Meg tell the owner that I shouldn't train Happy because I couldn't even run my own food. I didn't confront her on it, though. I wasn't big on confrontation.

Chef was whistling and the line guys were joking around about some girl they had both slept with.

"She is taking care of six hundred," I said, not sure I was entirely lying.

"Now *that's* a camper. That the same lady?" Kathy asked.

"Yeah."

"I swear, people can be so fucking rude," Kathy filled two glasses of water.

"She is still waiting for the other person to show," I said. I didn't consider her rude. Normally, campers annoyed me as badly as the next girl, but this woman somehow got the *okay*. I felt bad for her. Maybe it was that somewhat unjustified compassion I'd been feeling for the elderly lately.

A few minutes later I brought the dessert to the table for her. Happy was sitting down with her apron off and placed on the windowsill. They were talking about Iran, where Happy was born.

"I've been wanting to go back," the old lady said.

"Maybe we could go together sometime. I have family over there and we'd have a place to stay."

"Oh, that would be wonderful," the lady smiled.

"I chose the crème brulee for you," I said, placing the fries on the table between them, "it's my favorite."

"Thank you, dear, this is just perfect."

It dawned on me that she was by far the nicest woman I had ever served. I hoped I would be that nice when I became that age. I began to walk away, not having the heart to pull Happy away from her to get back to work, when she asked for one more ribeye dinner to take home.

"Oh, and a few boxes to take this other stuff home in," she finished.

"I can grab the boxes, Shell," Happy said as she stood up. Something seemed different about her suddenly. Maybe I was mistaken, but she seemed to stand straighter and speak with more confidence than only an hour before.

Back in the server alley, Kathy and Meg were both sipping coffee. "That guy is being a total pervert," Kathy said and nodded in the blue-capped man's direction. "He said a bunch of lame lines and then had the nerve to put his hand on my shoulder."

I looked at him, still standing alone at the bar and I felt sorry for him. If people were inherently good, what was it that left a man standing alone, desperate for human interaction at a bar on a Wednesday night?

"He touched you?" Meg asked, surprised.

"Yeah, creeper."

"Just ignore him and make sure you get walked out by someone tonight," I said. Sure, I liked to believe that we were all inherently good, but that didn't mean I would take any risks in the dark parking lot.

"Wouldn't it be funny if that man was the guy your old lady at six hundred is waiting for?" Meg laughed.

"What, because he's alone?" Kathy asked, annoyed.

"Yeah. They're both here alone. Can you picture them in bed?" Meg laughed out loud and Kathy almost choked on her coffee.

"Really, Meg?" was all I could get myself to say without losing my temper.

Meanwhile, Happy had come back and brought the ribeye and the check to the lady.

"Oh, look, speak of the devil," Kathy said as she walked out of the server alley.

The lady from 600 walked past us and out the door, bags of food hung on her arms.

I took care of my other tables and Happy bussed 600.

***

At the end of the shift, Kathy, Meg, Happy, and I were all rolling silverware when I asked Happy what had happened to the lady at 600.

"What do you mean?"

"She left. Did she like the crème brulee?"

"Oh yeah, we loved it."

"Who was she waiting for?" I asked, knowing Happy knew more than I did.

"Her husband—but get this—" Happy began.

"What kind of husband just leaves his wife to sit alone at a restaurant all night?" Kathy asked.

"The dead kind," Happy said.

"So she was waiting for her dead husband? She told you that?" Meg asked.

"Yes. Well, she said that every year on their anniversary they went to a new restaurant. This year they decided to try our place."

"People just keep getting more and more fucked up in this place," Meg said.

"But the guy is dead?" Kathy asked, confused.

"Yes," Happy reassured her.

"Then how did *they* decide to come here tonight?" Kathy leaned in closer toward Happy's chair.

"She says she still talks to him."

"That's crazy," Meg said.

"Well, she admitted that he doesn't talk back. But she said she can still feel him—feel his presence."

"She was a little nutty," Kathy laughed, "she was waving at the customers and the cars driving past."

"Oh, she did all of that for a laugh," Happy stood up for the woman. "I even waved at a few cars with her."

"You what?" Meg asked, disgusted.

"It's funny; they think they know you so they wave right back. It made me feel good," Happy smiled.

"So she knew she was waving at strangers?" Kathy asked, surprised.

"Yeah," Happy said.

I smiled as I felt a weight lifted from my chest.

"Well you sure spent enough time with her tonight," Meg said.

"Meg, don't," I said, not wanting to deal with the confrontation.

"Yeah, and...?" Happy straightened the collar of her shirt.

"Well, if you expect to keep your job here you can't be sitting around with the customers in the middle of the fucking dinner rush," Meg spat.

"I don't think I want to work here anymore," was Happy's response.

"Why? What happened?" I asked, concerned. I decided that I really liked Happy. She needed the money and this was where the money was.

"If I stay here, I am going to end up being that strip steak lady. I think I'd rather go back home," Happy said as she rolled the last piece of silverware. "I don't think I'm cut out for this."

"That's not true," I began, but didn't finish. I was beginning to wonder if any one of us was cut out for it.

"I wish you all the best and I'm lucky to have met you. We'll keep in touch. Shelly, I'd love for you to come and visit me sometime. I wish we would have met under better circumstances."

"Yeah, me too."

Happy stood up, gave me a hug goodbye, and as she walked out the door, I saw the flowers from table 600 wrapped in her long, black hair.

About the author:

Michelle has always been a fan of realistic fiction and continuously finds herself in awe of the undeniable power of language. You know when you read that paragraph or sentence that causes you to stop and breathe? Or that collection of words that takes you back to your grandma's living room, sitting on an old brown and white pleated couch, wrapped up in Grandma's quilt, and while you don't remember what you were doing on that couch, it doesn't matter? The words have brought you back to a specific moment and you acknowledge there is power in that.

Michelle first noticed the phenomenon as a young child in Spencer, Ohio when she was subject to meeting a few of her father's employees who did not know how to read. She fondly remembers these kind men asking her, a young child, to read warning labels and automobile pamphlets out loud and how important that made her feel. Looking back, she remembers the look in their eyes not as one of envy, but as one of astonishment. She noticed the phenomenon a second time when she was in junior high school and found herself with a gift of words. She had the ability to write a clear sentence that held her voice within the letters. This was around the time when she was introduced to James Hurst's "The Scarlett Ibis" and found herself crying uncontrollably for Doodle. They weren't simply tears, they were an emotion. A connection brought about through the author's words.

Most recently, though, Michelle has acknowledged the phenomenon in her Phoenix, Arizona classrooms. She places a strong focus on getting to know her students and teaching them how to place their own individual voice on the page. She works with students who have found themselves in a corner and are trying their hardest to reinvent. Michelle finds the ultimate power of language to be its ability to help these students re-enter the world and claim a new place within it. Language is a belief just as much as it is a skill.

"Waves" examines a time in Michelle's life when she had no idea what else the world had to hold. It examines what is going on in the "inside" during the madness of the outside. Michelle hopes that it leaves you with a sense of hope, but she will be happy and feel accomplished if it leaves you with a sense of anything at all.

Michelle wants to thank all of her friends and customers back at the restaurant in Lakewood, Ohio. Today, three years later, that world feels like a lifetime ago. She learned a lot of about herself and the person she wanted to become those few years taking orders and running food. She also wants to thank her fiancé, Brian, who joined her at a later time in her life but reminds her everyday why the struggle of leaving the service industry and entering the world of academia has been worth it. She is looking very forward to seeing how language will play in the next stage of her journey: New York City!

COLORCIDE
©2016 by JoAllen Bradham

This time the beginning was different. No boundary invaded. No fort fired upon, No ship sunk. Neither archduke shot nor bomb dropped. But the time was right for Armageddon. Special interest groups. Hate crimes. A school shooting each week. Terrorism and obsession about terrorists. Xenophobia. Each faction adamant. Compromise unthinkable. Each person wanted his or her end served regardless of the needs of millions. Politicians bickered around the clock and through the seasons. Campaigns had dissolved into slander, showboating, silliness, stupidity. Social media had become the means for transmitting social blindness. So we might say the feeling, the hair-trigger animosity of the times set off the carnage, but there was, also, a single inciting event. There always is. It started with an innocent question from a seventh-grade boy in the elementary civics class at Pleasant Heights Middle School. Billy Preston put up his hand and, when recognized, asked, "Ms. Goodman, does 'red state' mean that only red necks live there and 'blue state' mean that everyone there is what people call 'blue bloods'?" All kinds of sounds bubbled up around the cheerful, light-filled classroom—laughter, whys, groans that Billy had yet another question, sighs that they had to study civics in the first place. Ms. Goodman pointed to the map that was on the wall behind her. "This is the way it works, class." And she deftly explained about states voting Republican or Democratic and the way the colors had been taken, not too many elections ago, to stand for the majority vote and, thus, the categorizing image of its people.

Noises outside. Some color-mad gang is getting closer. All I have is a candle for light. Flashlight, too, but that's for escaping if I can, not for typing; a metal canister in which I hope I have time to insert this manuscript if a colorist breaks in. The bodies I had to step over in the hall didn't make it out.

Of course things didn't stop with the boy's question. Ms. Goodman barely had time to share a laugh with a few of her fellow teachers about the amusing, even endearing thing that had happened in seventh grade civics that day. Most children went home and told their parents that they had learned that only red necks lived in red states or they asked if they were blue bloods because they lived in a blue state. A few actually got the meaning right and raised questions about the up-coming election. Irate parents of those who got it wrong pulled themselves from in front of their televisions and started telephoning to other parents, to the school, the school board, the media, their churches, their representatives in Congress. Of course, the media picked it up. Viral in twelve hours.

This underground room of what was the Smithsonian's Museum of Natural History was the best I could manage with my leg bleeding and killers at my heels. Have to write fast. Suspect because I am known to use the forbidden terms, I have to leave a record. Someday survivors will want to know what has happened. Political observers in other, more moderate countries need a record from the inside. I've taken refuge before, here with this old manual typewriter, a grey Remington, the kind my mother used in her high school typing class. Thank God she did not live to see women of her generation slaughtered because they were styled "blue-haired ladies."

No electric power. Very few spots in the country still have energy. Very little infrastructure exists. Hence the typewriter that clicked and clacked in the '40s—during another war.

America was seething—with resentment, frustration, anger. It was an ugly and angry country. Red states and blue states had always been enemies, each longing to eradicate the other, but with the spreading of Billy's question, butchery started. "Call me a red neck! I'll show you." Bang. "So you think you're a blue blood? Tell me about it, your majesty." Bang.

For a few days the fights were between individuals. Many injuries, only a few deaths. A good bit of laughter from those who took a superior view. Then gangs formed, and the violence escalated. Anyone was fair game anywhere in the country. The least disagreement justified killing. Those wearing red or blue headscarves were preferred targets the first few days. After that, no blue or red headscarf was ever seen. No blue or red shirts or bandannas or baseball caps were seen.

> *Buildings all around the museum collapsed or burned, leaving only dark shells. This one endured, relatively intact except for holes in the venerable green dome. Everything in this room is gray, gloomy, monochromatic, barren. I'm wearing gray sweats, top and bottom (no hoodie attached), the uniform a few of us adopted a year ago to show neutrality. I've shaved my head. I try to shave my beard every day, but sometimes there is neither time nor place. Mostly gray, the beard is not much of a problem. To be colorless is the credo of the Resistance.*

As people looked around for more congenial places to live, where those of their own kind would be around them, providing a ring of protection, moving companies prospered. People in red neck states wanted to move so that without doing anything—except finding new jobs—they could become blue bloods. Those who could not move, fought. Gun sales soared as the President repeatedly pled for tighter gun control. At that point, however, rage was rampart, and guns came out of closets, guns were smuggled in, guns were manufactured in factories that claimed to be making heavy-duty plumbing pipes. Guns materialized by means of the incredible process of 3-D printing. Every day in every state there were shootouts, massacres, bloodbaths. Because police officers wore blue, they were inviting targets. Here was the solution to so-called police brutality. Police forces dwindled from murder and resignation. Being a police officer was the last thing anyone wanted. The President declared a 50-state state of emergency, called out the National Guard, enforced a gag order on the media. No one could speak or print "red state" or "blue state" because these terms were inflammatory and a threat to national security. But "Show Your Colors" became a rallying cry, its meaning different for each person using it.

> *A blast—must be the only remaining wall of the Space and Air Museum. Sudden draft. The one window, high up just below the ceiling, drops its dirty pane on the concrete floor a couple of yards from me. Another bomb—the fifth in the last hour. Dust settles all around me, dust that has been accumulating in this unused room for decades. Cough and keep typing.*

For decades, long before the Color Wars started, sports fanatics had torn down goal posts, trashed playing fields, destroyed trees on campuses, and spread wreckage on their football enemies, but that kind of violence soon registered as child's play. The red-blue war created an excuse for the mindless vengeful to kill supporters of teams and schools identified by the colors red and blue. Alabama's Crimson Tide took major hits. Some gang even went to the trouble of lining up dead bodies, head to toe, down the field. And generating the dead was easy. If a car had the university's decal on its windows, that driver was marked out as the red enemy. A new kind of Red Peril. The red of the Wisconsin Badger raised the wrath of the rabble, now there was nothing to restrain wrath or to encourage sportsmanship. Any shade of red qualified. Even the garnet of the University of South Carolina's Garnet and Black was a red flag. The state was decimated. Big Blue, stalwart Michigan, exacerbated those who hated blue. Support Big Blue quickly translated into eradication. The Wolverines were hunted beasts, even women innocently driving cars with the blue Wolverine emblazoned as a symbol. Big Blue, of course, meant Kentucky as well. Wildcats were in the crosshairs of a thousand rifles.

> *Water dripping. The last blast must have dislodged pipes. Water was about the only necessity that continued to be available and now it is part of the enemy here in the basement. I wonder about all the stuffed figures of animals on the floors above my head. The water will reach them. Post-extinction extinction.*

There is no explaining all this except the times in its myopic vision, its petty factions, the self-contained self-righteousness of practically every individual. Level-headed individuals saw what was happening, but their voices were like those of prophets crying in the wilderness. Every day hundreds of people quoted Yeats's line about the worst being filled with passionate intensity. The blood-dimmed tide was loose. No doubt about it, but because blood is red, what we said was limited. What we knew was fatal. It was not time for poetry or for prophets.

After six months, it was time for burning. Fires spread across Chicago, Atlanta, Richmond, Memphis, Houston, Los Angeles. All these lay in ruins. Skylines reimaged 9/11. Then things seemed to quiet down. The flames frightened some people. The millions displaced from these cities, the millions left homeless and with nothing to reestablish themselves shocked the nation into sympathy. Would FEMA do anything? Was arson in a civil rebellion a cause that justified federal funds to help those dispossessed? Different people—in what had been called different colored states—had different opinions. So nothing was done. The Color Wars were already winning.

Then the colors changed. *Red* and *Blue*, having been stricken from the vocabulary, left a gap, but not for long. "Black Power," a thousand voices screamed in a rabid recapitulation of the 1960s cry. "Black Lives," a million echoed. Then almost antiphonally: "White supremacy, white supremacy, white supremacy." And the black-white race war detonated, fueled and seemingly justified by the on-going red-blue colorcide. Atrocities, barbarism.

Cities in the South burned first: Jackson, Columbia, Nashville, Birmingham, Montgomery, but by the end of the first year, the red-orange flame fingers reached into the sky and ignited the passions of Detroit, Ann Arbor, Seattle, Tulsa, Denver, Portland, Topeka, Philadelphia, New York, San Francisco, Washington, D.C.

> *Another blast. Three in a row. Something new is happening outside. Shield the candle so I can keep typing with one hand. I want to get the facts down—in brief at least—before I try to escape. I've lost a good bit of blood. My left trouser leg is soaked. More water. Not just dripping now, rushing. Sounds as if it comes from two directions. But this building, housing a rich past since 1910, is sturdy, meant to withstand onslaught. Now kill or be killed is part of its natural history.*

Although Washington had burned, many of the legislators survived and they tried to meet and argue about bringing order out of chaos. There was some talk of allocating federal funds to set up "cities of preference" so that each person or family might move to a location reserved exclusively for residents of the same persuasion. This was the promise of personal, political, and racial independence, which some shouted was guaranteed by the Constitution, but a handful of still responsible individuals, led by the senior senators from Kansas and Missouri, recalled that this kind of allocation had been tried in the designation of slave states and free states as settlers moved west and wished to turn territories into states. And you see how that ended, they stressed. Others, from both North and South, picking up on the slave-state/free-state fiasco pointed to the more obvious failure of the Civil War, which also tried to grant personal and political independence to a region. The issue of States Rights came up, the problems of secession, the inequality of wealth and of natural resources in different geographic areas. The plan to set up "cities of preference" was dropped. No alternative emerged.

Senator J. J. Gulls of Alaska, known for his eloquence, begged for unity, enjoined his colleagues to set aside party and regional differences, to forget personal ambition and reelection, and do all they could to save the country. He said too much. In the heat of the moment, he exhorted: "At a time like this, we have to put aside the problems we have been wrestling with, things like global warming and drilling for oil. We cannot invoke a green world if there is to be no world at all."

Madness spewed out of every newspaper, every TV channel, every computer. Social media bayed with ferocity. Taking their cue from Senator Gulls, millions chanted: "Drill here. Drill now." Wherever streets still existed, they were filled with protestors advocating immediate drilling for oil. Wiping out those who did not agree with drilling was part of the strategy. In Oklahoma there were cases of actually boiling dissenters in oil—someone must have been reading up on the Middle Ages. Less opposition translated into greater opportunity. Others gloried in the chance to proclaim that global warming was a myth perpetrated by anti-American enmity to big business and ready profits. These demonstrators chanted "Global Warming—No Such Thing." The issue was green, and the third phase of the Color Wars was green. Red, blue, black, white, green. The bruise that obliterated America.

Water is dripping through the ceiling. I move my candle out of the path of the water. Just a little more and I'll put the papers in the canister and carry it to safety. If I can still get out. I've signed off many an article for one paper or another. This may be the final sign-off.

By the end of the second year, only about half the airports in the country were still functioning and planes still flying. Airlines that had any of the five death-dealing colors on the bodies of the planes had painted them over in a battleship gray. They rose and landed like grim, gigantic birds that had molted and had little expectation of growing new feathers. People were flying out to anywhere. Those who had passports and money packed up and left, willing to go anywhere that would take them as refugees. England and Ireland were the most sought after destinations because of the language, but both quickly realized there was no way to effect reverse colonization. Tight quotas were set and maintained. Australia let in more. There was plenty of open space for immigrants who had not checked what life on the Outback was like.

Millions assumed they could fill up the gas tanks and drive to Canada, but service stations and fuel became increasingly scarce. Canada closed its border after so many thousands crossed and attempted to settle. Mexico, surprised at the speed at which the wall came down and the patrols stopped, assigned men to stand at the boundary and wave drivers in with the national flag. The country welcomed those who showed the money and drove good cars. Small boats offloaded the brave on the shores of Cuba. The process looked as if news films from the past were being shown in reverse. Balmy and romantic Caribbean islands, once the escapist's tropical paradise, took on new identity: desperation destination. Cruise ships—those still in business—saw the possibility of increasing revenue. They loaded passengers for European ports, but after the first three big ships found harbor, the others replayed the futile voyages of the ships carrying Jews escaping Hitler. No port would admit them.

Also by the end of the second year, outside agitators were in the action, helping with slaughter, making devastation the norm. Shouting that the time of Arab world-dominance had come, the outsiders urged the utter defeat of all things American, the obliteration of Western corruption.

Water or strong men are pressing into the old wooden door I locked behind me. I've heard running boots.

I know I should give documentation, examples, development, but there is no time. This is an on-the-front report from one embedded, not with troops, but within the last hours of hopelessness. European historians can put the pieces together and supply footnotes and references.

When the third year of the Color Wars began, no one really knew much outside of his or her immediate areas. Small rural communities functioned best for a while but with no trucks or trains bringing in goods and no way to get their crops to a market, these places began to fade and follow the cities into desolation. The towers for cell phones, the fiber optics for computers and TVs, the electric grids in all the metropolitan areas had ceased to function. Wi-fi? As if it had never been. Exploding chemical plants introduced chemical warfare. Looting of the CDC in Atlanta created the fear of germ warfare, but nothing happened. Unless the living have incubated germs that in time will work their ways. Cities that had not burned still looked like cities but only cut-out cities or cities that might be gigantic stage sets that had to stand but offer neither light nor sound. Cities, as still as pictures of ancient cities found only in the pages of history books, or full scale models that a city planner might use to....

About the author:

My debut novel, *Some Personal Papers*, won the 1994 Breakthrough Award in Southern and Southwestern Fiction with publication by the *Texas Review Press*. This edition won the 1996 Townsend Award, Georgia's top fiction prize. *Black Belt Press* (now *River City Publishing*) then issued both paperback and hardback editions. The Black Belt edition won for me the 2000 Georgia Writer of the Year Award in Fiction.

THE HERO OF LOST CAUSES
©2016 By Phillip Frey

Robert Emmet was born in Ireland in 1778. Upon his twenty-third year he became angry over British rule. It then took him two years to recruit an army of farmers, shepherds and friends. When the moment of rebellion finally came, there was a miscue and a lot of confusion. As a result, the British captured Robert Emmet and executed him in 1803.
Robert Emmet quickly became a romantic figure to the Irish people; to this day referred to as "The Hero of Lost Causes."

Riverhead is at the far end of Long Island with a bay to the Atlantic. On Memorial Day, the town begins to fill with vacationers who have come to take advantage of the fishing season. When Labor Day arrives, the townspeople return to their quiet, homespun lives.

A number of decades ago, in this predominately Irish township, the locals would gather twice a month during the off-season and listen to tales of Irish history and folklore. Stories of struggle and courage, and of sprites and leprechauns, told by retired fireman Kevin Michael Emmett.

There was only one thing about Kevin that troubled the locals: Kevin's insistent belief in his kinship to the 18th-century Irish patriot Robert Emmet.

The Riverhead locals doubted that Kevin Michael Emmett was a direct descendant, especially since Kevin's surname had a second T at the end.

Kevin had answered this many times: "When me and the folks come over, Immigration added the extra T, they did, and that's that."

Kevin had named his son Robert after the Irish hero, feeling in his bones that someday the lad would become a hero and give credence to the lineage.

After retiring from the fire department, old Kevin bought a 40-foot fishing vessel and opened a fishing charter business, summers only.

The office was in a trailer just off the marina parking lot. Labor Day had come and gone. It was on a Saturday morning that Kevin was at his desk with a glass of Irish whiskey. His son, Robert, sat on the sofa, flipping through a fishing tackle magazine.

"Hey, Pop," he said, "I'm going to be thirty next month."

"Your dear departed mother'd be prouda ya, she would."

"For what?"

Old Kevin looked into his drink. "Makin' it t'thirty, safe and sound."

His son stretched out on the sofa and thought about the hero Robert Emmet, a hero at twenty-five. He sat up then. "Pop, you've proven the lineage. You're a hero of a lost cause—me."

"You're no lost cause and I'm no hero. Robert Emmet's in your blood, he is, and one day we'll be sure t'know it."

The phone rang. "Don't answer, Pop, might be a charter."

"Ehh, nobody here to fish off-season." Kevin picked it up. "Emmett's Charter," he answered. "Poseidon? Musta got the wrong...oh...oh...yep, uh-huh. Stay put a minute."

Kevin covered the mouthpiece. "It's the Poseidon Cremation Society of West Hampton," he told his son in a whisper. "Got a cracked hull and a service in three hours. Says give us three hundred for a half-hour anchor time."

Robert set his magazine down. "Not bad for throwing ashes to the wind."

"Saturday—got folks comin' t'listen to the Big Fella story."

"No problem. I'll take her out, I can handle it," Robert said with quiet authority.

Kevin gave his son a nod of approval. Robert's quiet authority is what gave Kevin all the more reason to hang on to his dream. His son sounded like a hero.

Kevin uncovered the phone and was transferred to a Mr. Evans.

Two hours later the funeral procession rolled in. Kevin and his son came out of the trailer as fourteen mourners got out of four cars, somber men and women in drab clothing.

Kevin eyed the hearse, thinking it a mighty respectful way to carry a jar of ashes. Mr. Evans slid out of the hearse. He was on the short side and had a stern hatchet face, neatly barbered white hair, and wore a suit as black as the hearse.

Old Kevin introduced himself to Mr. Evans. That was when Mr. Evans smelled whiskey. "Mr. Emmett," he said, "are you the one who'll be taking us out?"

Kevin heard the accusation in his voice. "It'll be my son here, Robert. Sober as British Parliament."

Robert and Mr. Evans shook hands, Robert giving him a smile; the smile actually meant for Kevin. Robert knew his father thought British Parliament was a house of drunks.

Mr. Evans gave Robert the once-over. Robert's tall, strong-looking figure and steady dark eyes reassured him.

The mourners stayed in a bunch alongside the hearse. Kevin and his son led Mr. Evans into the trailer. After Robert showed Mr. Evans the course he had charted, Mr. Evans joined old Kevin at his desk and wrote out a check.

Robert's eyes shifted to an office window. He gazed at the mourners, struck suddenly by the most beautiful woman he had ever seen. She looked up and caught his stare.

He turned from the window, a bit embarrassed, her green eyes stamped in memory as he heard Mr. Evans: "I'll ready the pallbearers and you can walk us aboard."

"Ehh, pallbearers did you say?" old Kevin asked.

"Oh, didn't I—this isn't a cremation," Mr. Evans explained. "Burials at sea are unusual but the deceased had requested it in his will. We'll strap the casket and lower it from the gin pole."

"Ehh, yep, I see," Kevin muttered. Then said, "Don't matter much, long as it's legal."

"Oh, it's legal all right," Mr. Evans told him. "Beyond the three-mile limit."

Kevin nodded and his son asked, "Half-hour anchor time?"

"Yes, Robert, same as cremations."

A few minutes later Mr. Evans stood with Kevin and Robert at the starboard side of the docked 40-footer, christened *Robert Emmet*. Mr. Evans eyed the forward hull and said to Kevin, "I see you named your boat after your son, but why is there only one T at the end of the name?"

"Ah," Kevin responded brightly. "Me *ship* is named after the Irish patriot Robert Emmet. Do you know of him?"

"No," Mr. Evans said with little interest, "can't say that I do."

"A grand bit of history that goes back to the early days of the struggle. A time when—"

"Pop," Robert interrupted, "we have to step aside."

Six men bore the casket by them, then up the railed ramp to the deck. Robert saying, "Okay, Pop, we've got to get aboard." Then to Mr. Evans, "Follow me and hold the rail."

Once aboard, Robert spread a tarp behind the stern's three fighting chairs. The pallbearers gently set the casket down on it. Robert folded the electronic ramp against the hull, and then threw the spring lines down to his father. On his way to the helm he exchanged a glance with the green-eyed, mournful beauty and felt as though he had been zapped.

Kevin called out from dockside: "Good sailin', me boy!" He watched the *Robert Emmet* glide across the bay and out to sea, and then returned to the trailer where his whiskey awaited him.

An hour or so later a portion of the marina parking lot was filled with families, seated in the folding chairs that Kevin had supplied. They were listening to the beginning of Kevin's Big Fella story, the story of the Irish patriot Michael Collins.

From the side of the trailer a ship-to-shore speaker squawked, followed by, "Hey, Pop, are you there?"

"Ehh, me apologies," Kevin said to the crowd. "Be back in a minute."

"No worry," Mrs. McGinty called out, "we'll be settin' up the food table."

Kevin went into the trailer. On the ship-to-shore he answered his son and heard him say, "Got an emergency. Said the prayers, winched the casket down, released it and it won't sink."

"She's afloat!"

"No," Robert told him. "I gaffed it. Tore it up a bit, but got it back aboard. Everyone's pretty upset, especially Mr. Evans, about not having weighed it down enough. So we need a favor."

"Ehh, sure—sure."

"Mr. Evans says bricks. We'd have to come in for them and go out again. So I thought you could go to McGinn's, get a big load of them. Then borrow one of Fred's speedboats and meet us out here. The *Cigarette*'s the fastest."

"Jesus-Mary, I'm in no condition to go speedin' about."

"C'mon, Pop, set your mind to it, you can do it. There's a copy of the chart on your desk."

"Ehh, yep, so there is, so there is…. Well now, no sense turnin' a half-hour anchor time into a whole day."

"Thanks, Pop. See you soon."

Moored out at sea, Robert stood in the flying bridge. He turned and there she was. Her dark hair shivered in the wind and her green eyes gleamed in the sunlight.

"Excuse me, I don't mean to disturb you," she said in a timber that sent Robert's blood rushing.

His quiet authority weakened. "No, it's, it's all right."

"I came to thank you for saving my grandfather's casket. If you hadn't, my grandmother might have jumped in after it."

Robert glanced down at the deck where the old woman stood, held steady by a relative. "She really wouldn't have, would she?"

"Granny's very old and out of balance, mentally and physically, what with the passing of Grandfather, and what's happened with the casket, along with the rocking of the boat."

"I'm sorry."

"Not your fault." She pointed down toward the stern. "Why do those three chairs have straps?"

"They're fighting chairs, bolted to the deck. The straps stop you from getting pulled in when you hook a swordfish, marlin, anything big."

"Would you mind if we strapped Granny in one? When she sits on the side benches she falls over."

"No, I don't mind."

"I heard Mr. Evans call you Robert, so it's Robert, is it?"

Asking him this he heard a bit of an Irish lilt. He glanced down at her left hand and saw no wedding ring. Barely able to speak, he looked into her shining eyes and whispered, "Robert."

"Are you all right?" she asked softly.

"Yes, yes, I'm fine, it was just a..." and he shrugged it off. "And your name is...?"

"Eileen," she said with a light smile.

***

Back in Riverhead, the portly, round-faced James McGinn was where he always was, in his cushioned chair behind the counter. "Ya want old or new?"

"Old," said Kevin, "and I'm in a hurry."

"More costly," McGinn warned him.

"Old bricks more than new? You cheatin' me, James McGinn?"

"Old's got the antique look. Hard to come by with no cracks. Wha'cha ya usin' 'em fer?"

"Ehh, ya wouldn't believe it. Gimme the new."

"How many?"

"'Nough to keep, ehh...big heavy box at the bottom'a the sea."

McGinn closed an eye and glared at him with the other. "Ya ain't done murder, have ya, Kevin Michael Emmett?"

"I'll give ya murder if ya don't gimme me bricks!"

James McGinn pressed the intercom, called for his son's help, and then hefted his big body from the cushioned chair. "Come along, then."

Out in the brick-and-lumber yard, McGinn and his burly son loaded the bed of Kevin's pickup with two hundred pounds of new bricks. Because of McGinn's persistence, Kevin buckled and told him the troublesome casket story.

When done with the loading, Kevin paid and drove off. McGinn returned to his cushioned chair behind the counter, grinned and said to himself, "Could happen to nobody but the likes of Kevin Michael Emmett."

Kevin had already called, the *Cigarette* tanked and ready when he got there. He backed his pickup down to the dock where Fred Foote stood in his Riverhead police uniform. The dark blue of the uniform complimented his fiery eyes. Fiery due to the red cracks and hues caused by his late-night carousing. He was a likable, handsome man, always respectful to the townspeople.

Fred Foote could see that Kevin was a trifle off balance. He poured him a coffee from his thermos and proceeded to transfer the bricks to the speedboat. He did it alone while Kevin sat on a piling sipping the warm drink. This did not bother Fred in the least: he had been raised on Kevin's stories and would have done anything for him.

Finished loading the *Cigarette*, Fred asked Kevin what he was going to do out there with all those bricks.

Kevin gave up, thinking the whole town might as well know about it, and he again told about the unsinkable casket.

***

Past three o'clock and the *Robert Emmet* was still moored out at sea. The weather had taken a turn and the water was choppy. Granny, strapped in one of the fighting chairs, stared blankly out over the stern. The casket lay on the tarp behind her. Mr. Evans paced alongside it. The mourners on deck felt the ocean chill and passed it on to Mr. Evans with their eyes.

Robert and Eileen appeared from below, each carrying a pile of sweaters. Robert telling her they had been knitted by the locals for the christening of the ship, and had doubled as a gift in return for his father's stories.

Robert and Eileen handed out the sweaters. To get one over Granny, they had to unstrap and re-strap her. Mr. Evans helped with Granny, and that was when he spotted the speedboat.

"There he is!"

Everyone gathered at the stern and gazed entranced at the seawater that sprayed upward on either side of Kevin, who stood at the wheel. Eileen touched Robert's arm and said, "Your father looks like he has wings."

Kevin slowed the *Cigarette* toward the transom, wondering about the bound-up old woman who faced him. "Good woman," he hollered upward, "has me son turned pirate!"

Eileen smiled and Granny made a guttural sound. Eileen kept her eyes on Robert as he directed his father starboard, threw him a line, and then climbed over the rail. His father's words still with her, she saw Robert as a pirate, and she felt a sudden warmth.

Eileen went starboard and leaned over to see him step into the speedboat. Robert turned up to her. Their eyes met and held steady.

Old Kevin caught the moment. "Yep," he said softly.

Father and son tossed the bricks upward one-by-one to Mr. Evans and the others. There were a few misses but no one was hurt. When done, Kevin and Robert climbed aboard. Behind Granny, Mr. Evans opened the casket and the bricks were stacked evenly around the body. Granny heard the clink of brick against brick and moaned quietly.

Eileen unstrapped her and held her upright alongside the open casket of body and bricks. Granny stood in near-catatonia, and for the second time they all paid their last respects.

Mr. Evans closed the casket. Robert tied it up, swung the heavy load out over port, and then winched it downward. To the tune of its creaking, Mr. Evans recited Last Rites for the second time. He then nodded to Robert who pulled the release.

Everyone leaned over the port rail and witnessed the dark box vanish into the depths. Old Kevin muttered, "Done at last," then went to the helm and pulled up anchor.

Robert and Eileen led Granny back to the fighting chair, strapped her in, and then joined Kevin at the helm. Eileen studied Robert's hands as he turned the keys and flipped the switches. The engines started with a deep rumble, followed by a horrific shriek. "Like the cry of the banshee," as Kevin would later describe it.

Robert cut the engines. He and his father hurried to the stern with Eileen. Granny gave out another shriek and everyone followed her stare to see the deceased riding the waves like a wooden plank. All stood shocked at the sight.

"Christ sake!" Mr. Evans cried out, repeatedly pounding a fist on the rail. "Why did I—it's an airtight casket—you can't open—damn it—damn it!"

Granny passed out. Her mind wanted no more of it.

The body rose and fell in the waves. Someone shouted, "He's getting away!" and they all tried to get each other to do something.

Robert leaned over the rail so as not to lose sight of him. The ship listed and he went overboard. On his way down he hollered, "*Cigarette!*"

Eileen kept a fearful watch on Robert swimming out toward her grandfather. Mr. Evans and the others were stunned silent, the ultimate confusion being Robert's call for a cigarette.

Old Kevin raced across deck to get to the *Cigarette* down on the starboard hull. He tripped on the tarp and slid headfirst into the bulwark. He was out like a light, the only one who knew what Robert had meant when he called out for the *Cigarette*.

Mr. Evans followed Eileen to Kevin's aid. They knelt alongside him as he came to and mumbled, "Boat...speed."

With realization, Eileen got to her feet and climbed overboard. She hurried down the ladder and into the *Cigarette* where she frantically eyed the dash. She prayed for luck, turned the key and flipped one of the switches. It started.

She fumbled with the line and got it untied. Looking under the dash, there was no accelerator pedal. "Dang it!" she blurted out. Eyes back on the dash, she saw a handle that looked like a gearshift. She gripped it tightly and pushed it forward.

The *Cigarette* accelerated with a jolt and scraped alongside the hull. Eileen worked the wheel, got control finally and took off.

Aboard the *Robert Emmet*, Mr. Evans helped Kevin to his feet, and then to the stern. They watched with the others, Robert nearing the deceased, both moving farther out, sinking and rising between the waves.

Eileen raced the *Cigarette* around in wide circles, and then at last achieved a near-straight line.

Old Kevin made his way to the helm of the *Robert Emmet*, pulled anchor, started the engines and turned the ship.

Robert struggled against the rough waters that tumbled him every which way. Forced beneath the surface, he saw a blur of black and caught hold of it. He dug his fingers in, pulled himself upward, wrapping his arms around what turned out to be Eileen's grandfather.

Above the surface now, Robert choked and coughed into the cold and salty black suit and thanked heaven for the dead life preserver.

Eileen pulled the throttle handle down. The *Cigarette* slowed to an idle and rocked on the waves. She reached out and grabbed Robert's hand, his other held tight around her grandfather's belt. Robert looked up into her green eyes and said against the wind, "We've only known each other a few hours, but...."

"But what?" she said with a smile, seawater splashing them both.

They were interrupted by the *Robert Emmet* pulling up for the final rescue. The soaked body of the departed was hoisted aboard, Robert and Eileen alone now in the *Cigarette*. There was no more to say as they embraced, lips touching, both knowing that today would be the beginning of their lives together.

When Eileen finally climbed up from the *Cigarette*, she went to the fighting chair where Granny had just regained consciousness, Granny unaware of her husband drying out behind her on the tarp.

Eileen told her that Grandpa had been saved and they would be heading back to shore. Then said, "I'm sorry to have to tell you this, but we'll have to go through this again tomorrow."

Granny's eyes rolled with the ship.

Robert had secured the *Cigarette* to the hull and was now climbing aboard. As soon as old Kevin saw him, he danced a jig on deck, everyone thinking he had cracked under the pressure. He danced over to his son, hugged and kissed him, something he had not done since Robert was a boy.

"Me lad," he whispered in Robert's ear, "you went and saved a dead man!" He turned from Robert and shouted into the wind, "If ever there was a lost cause!"

The locals never again questioned the father and son's linage to the Irish patriot Robert Emmet.

About the author:

Phillip Frey grew up in Cleveland, Ohio, where he performed as a child actor at The Cleveland Playhouse. He later moved to New York, where he performed with Joseph Papp's New York Shakespeare Festival. This was followed by performing for one season as a member of The Repertory Theater of Lincoln Center.

With a change of interest Phillip wrote, directed and edited three short films, all of which had international showings, including the New York Film Festival.

With yet another change of interest, Phillip moved to Los Angeles where he became a produced screenwriter. Now more recently, he has turned to prose with the books "Dangerous Times" and "Hym and Hur." To see more about these books, please visit www.phillipfrey.com.

"The Hero of Lost Causes" is Phillip Frey's first publication of a short story. He wholeheartedly thanks Scribes Valley for this distinction.

www.ingramcontent.com/pod-product-compliance
Lightning Source LLC
Chambersburg PA
CBHW071249130626

46556CB00003B/1238